CW00498661

THE BOOSEY BRASS METHOD

series editor:

CHRIS MORGAN

trombone 𝄢 book 1

BOOSEY & HAWKES

London · New York · Berlin · Sydney

Series editor: Chris Morgan

Chris Morgan began teaching in 1974 and has been committed to instrumental teacher and curriculum development since 1979, when he was appointed Head of Woodwind for the Inner London Education Authority (ILEA). Subsequent posts have included Head of Instrumental Services with ILEA, Director of Instrumental Teacher Training at Guildhall School of Music & Drama, London, responsibility for professional and curriculum development with Cornwall Education Authority, and as a provider of professional development programmes with the Associated Board of the Royal Schools of Music, Guildhall School of Music & Drama and numerous music services in the UK and elsewhere. He is currently co-director of Music and Dance Education, based in Cornwall.

Trombone specialist: Peter Gane, Head of Wind and Percussion, Guildhall School of Music & Drama, London
Brass consultant: Ian Lowes, Head of Composition, Bryanston School and CTABRSM brass mentor

Boosey & Hawkes acknowledges the assistance of the Guildhall School of Music & Drama in developing the curriculum framework used in this series.

Feeling the Rhythm activities by Pat Hickman, co-director of Music and Dance Education
Music setting by Artemis Music Ltd.
Illustrations by Valerie Hill
Recordings by CN Productions
Cover design by Electric Echo
Printed by Halstan & Co. Ltd., Amersham, Bucks., England

INTRODUCTION

The Boosey Woodwind and Brass Method is designed to be used in lessons and when you play your instrument between lessons. To get the most out of the book, work through it with your teacher, playing the music and doing the activities. The CDs will help you between lessons - it contains performances and backing tracks of most of the pieces in the book, as well as listening activities.

At the end of the book you will find checklists for each stage. These help you to keep track of what you have learned. When you reach the end of a stage, fill in the checklist with your teacher. If there are gaps, try to finish the activities before you go on to the next stage. The activities are designed to help you explore music and improve as a musician.

Remember, different people learn at different speeds. Try not to rush. Work at a pace that feels comfortable. That way you will learn faster, and enjoy playing more.

This book is divided into nine sections - a "basics" section and eight stages. The basics pages (4-7) are orange and contain information about your instrument (how to hold it, how to look after it) and exercises to help you get started. Keep referring back to this section to remind yourself how to do these correctly.

Stages 1 to 8 teach you how to play the trombone and how to make music come alive. In addition to pieces to play, there are many different types of activities for you to do. The icons below have been designed to help you. Each one has a different meaning.

Warm-ups - have you warmed up properly? To help you do this, each stage begins with warm-up exercises.

Breathing activity - are you breathing in the right way? See page 5 for more about this.

Feel the rhythm - this could mean clapping, moving, counting, singing or two of these things at once.

Clap or sing - there are some tunes and activities for clapping or singing, and others which you clap or sing first, then play.

Write or record - sometimes you will find activities which include writing things down or making a recording.

Ensemble - this icon means you can play the piece with anyone learning from any *Boosey Brass* or *Boosey Woodwind* book.

Use the CDs - select the track number in the icon. You may have to listen - or you may be asked to sing or play along.

Answer a question - or solve a puzzle, or think about something in a different way.

Using the CD

Books in the *Boosey Woodwind and Brass Method* include two CDs:

- **performance CD** - use this CD to hear complete performances of the music
- **backing CD** - use this CD to play along with

Both CDs contain the same music so the track listings are identical. Each recording begins with clicks to show you at what speed to play.

You will also find tuning notes on the CD - **F** on track 2 and **low B♭** on track 23.

Additional web resources, including backing tracks, extra pieces and activities are available for *The Boosey Woodwind and Brass Method.* Visit **www.boosey.com** for further information.

Parts of a trombone

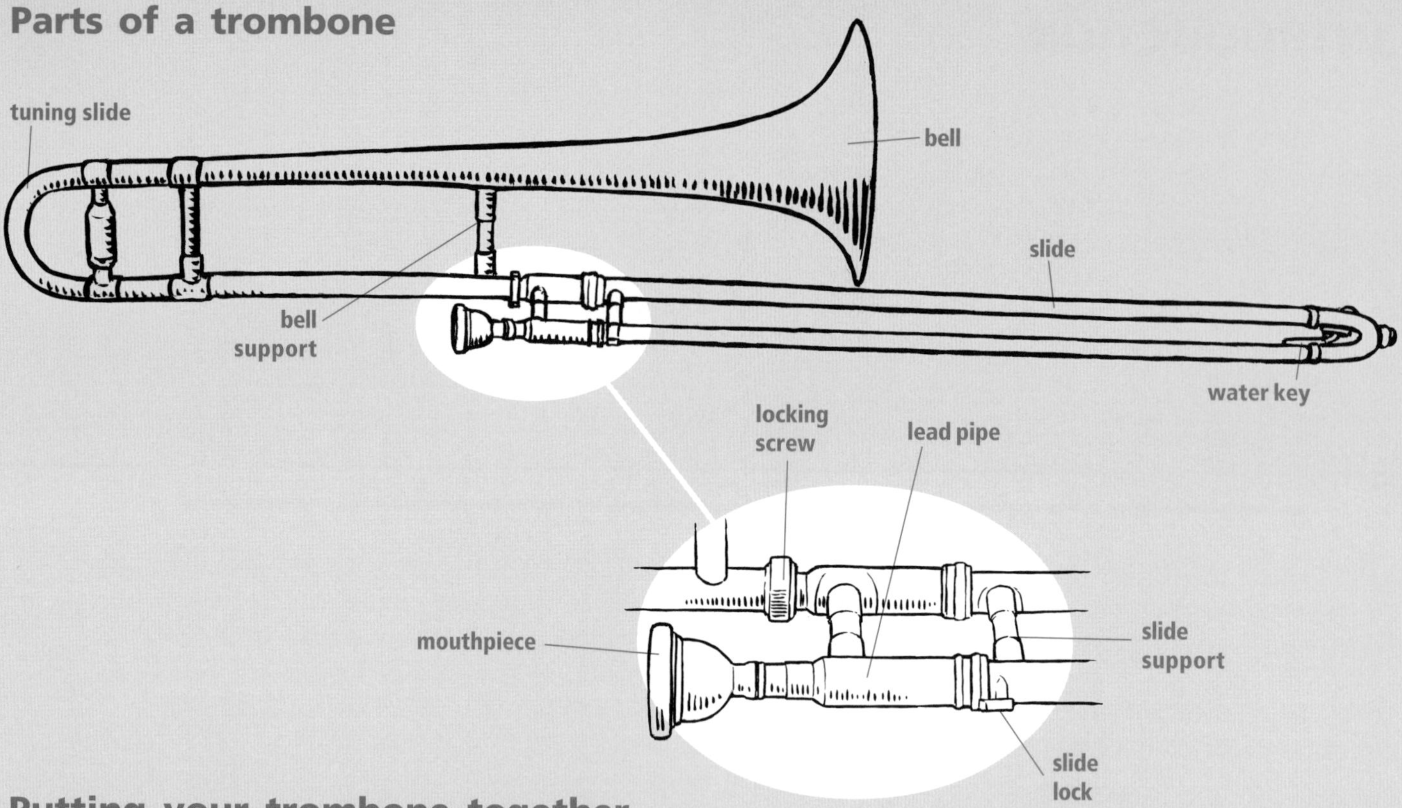

Putting your trombone together

Ask your teacher for more help with this. Lay your instrument case somewhere safe before opening the lid - on a table or on the floor. Make sure that your hands are clean as dirt can damage your trombone. Be careful not to drop or bang your instrument - brass is soft and dents easily.

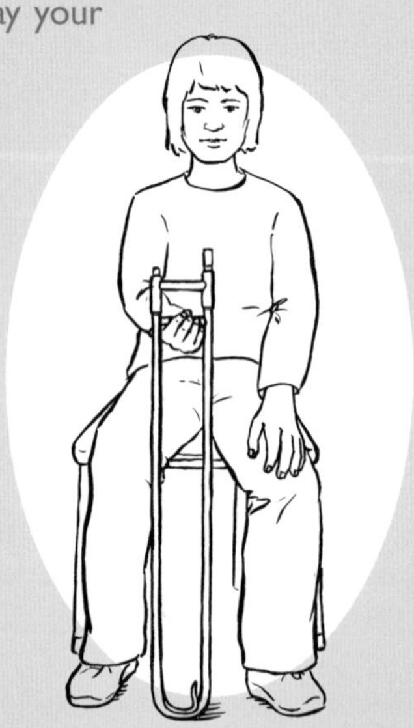

Remove the slide from the case, checking the slide lock is on. While seated, hold the slide in your right hand with the curve resting on the floor and the tallest tube on your left.

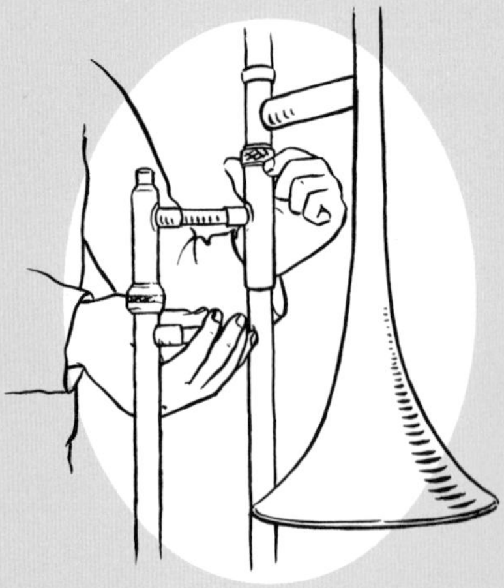

Remove the bell section from the case and, with your left hand, place it on the tallest tube with the bell facing away from you, forming a right angle or slightly less. Make sure that the bell and slide are not too close together. Join the two parts by turning the screw until it is finger tight.

Take the mouthpiece, place it in the instrument and gently twist it into position. Avoid banging it into the leadpipe.

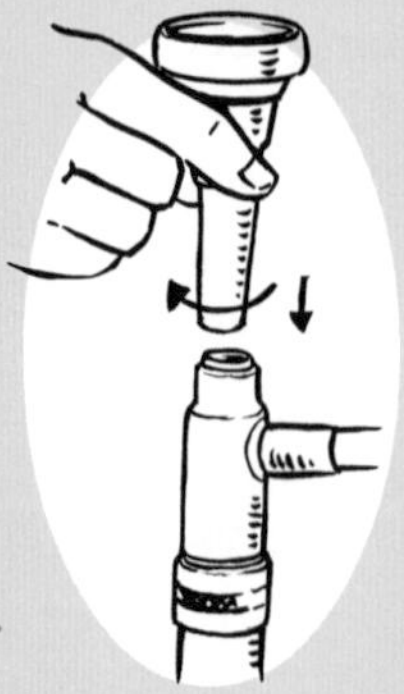

Holding your trombone

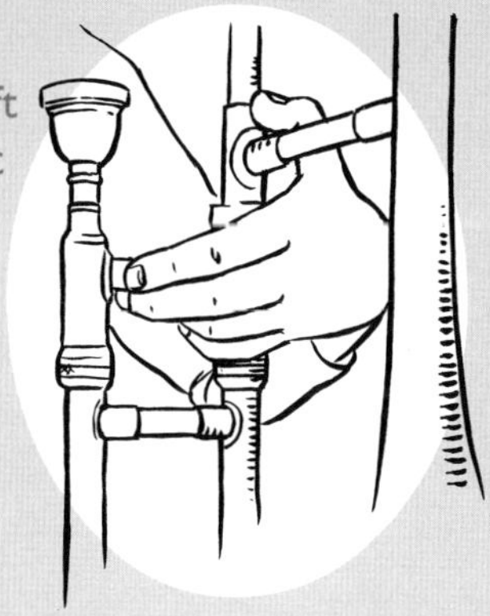

Position the thumb of your left hand across the bell support and stretch the rest of your hand across the slide support. It is your left hand that holds and supports the trombone.

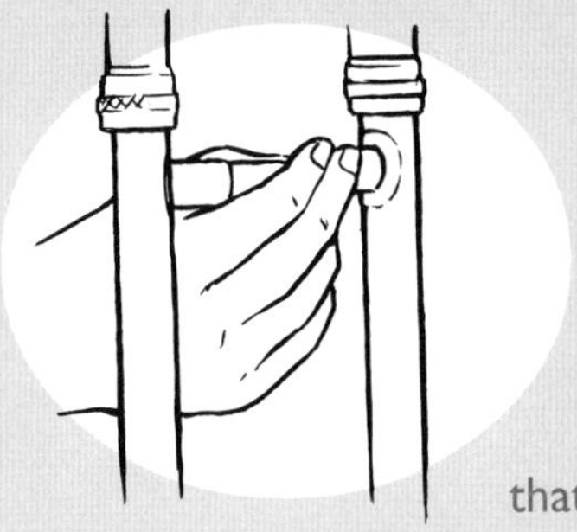

With your right hand, hold the slide section (initially with the lock on) between your thumb and first two fingers. Make sure you are still sitting upright and bring your trombone up to your lips. Your left forearm and hand should work together with the wrist set in position, but make sure that they are not tense.

The trombone should not touch your head or shoulder when you are playing. Keep your elbows slightly away from your body.

How to stand or sit when playing

When playing your trombone, you should stand or sit upright, but keep your body balanced and relaxed. Put both feet flat on the floor, slightly apart. Always bring the instrument to your lips – never take your lips to the mouthpiece.

If you are sitting, use a chair without arms and sit on the front half of the chair. If you are using a music stand, make sure it is at the right height for you.

Your upper body should remain the same if you are standing or sitting and your arms should be realxed and not held tightly into your body.

Always hold your trombone up and avoid pointing the bell at the floor. If you feel tired and can't hold your instrument up, stop and have a rest.

Breathing

When you play your trombone, you will need to breathe differently from usual. At first it is a good idea to practise breathing without holding your instrument.

Breathing in (inhaling)
Open your throat, as if you are yawning. Take a deep breath in through your mouth. When you breathe in, your shoulders should stay still. Your stomach and your whole ribcage will spread outwards. (If you put your hands gently on your stomach as you breathe in, you will feel this).

Breathing out (exhaling)
Breathe out slowly from your lower stomach. Keep the flow of air steady - imagine you are blowing up a balloon or blowing bubbles. When you breathe out, your cheeks should not puff out. Your stomach and ribcage will move inwards again as you breathe out.

Forming an embouchure and making a sound

An embouchure (say "om - boo - sure") is the position of your lips, teeth, tongue and cheeks that you use when playing. Everybody's embouchure is different – ask your teacher for more help.

With your teeth in line (or as near in line as is comfortable) but slightly apart, firm your lips against your teeth. Take a deep breath and blow out through the centre of your lips, without making a sound. Be careful not to puff out your cheeks

Try to ensure that the air comes straight out, as if blowing out a candle. Try this again but gradually move your lips closer together so that they vibrate making a **buzz**. This is the basis of producing a sound on your trombone.

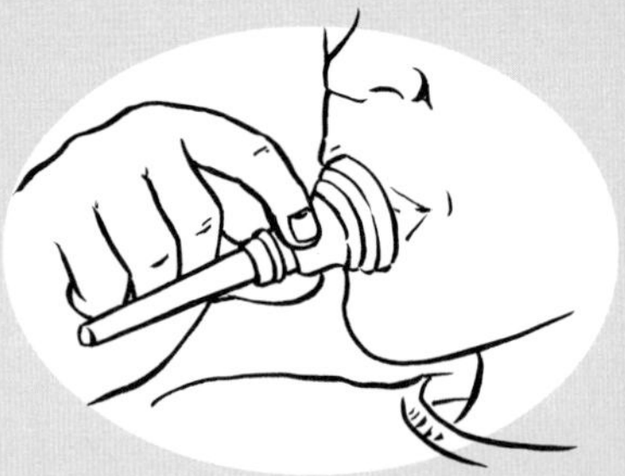

Mouthpiece buzzing

Take your mouthpiece without the instrument and hold it with your thumb and forefinger. Moisten your lips then place it lightly against the centre of your mouth and make the buzzing sound into it. Buzz in exactly the same way as without the mouthpiece.

Breathe as before but through the corners of your mouth so that the mouthpiece stays on your lips. Keep a steady buzz and avoid puffing your cheeks out. Keep the mouthpiece pressure to a minimum (your lips are a cushion for the mouthpiece to rest on).

98 You can hear what a mouthpiece buzz sounds like on track 98 of the CD.

To make a clean start to each buzz, use your **tongue** and imagine saying the word "**too**". The tip of your tongue should be touching the bottom edge of your top teeth when you start to make each sound.
Practise this tongued buzz several times.

buzz	rest	buzz
buzz	rest	buzz

Replace the mouthpiece in the instrument, bring it to your lips, take a deep breath and breathe out through the instrument, making the buzz at the same time. You should have your first note.

Practise holding steady notes for as long as you can. Also play long notes broken up into shorter sounds by using your tongue to "**too**" the start of each note

2 You have probably discovered it is possible to play a few different types of buzzing sounds and notes. Practise the note that you can play when your embouchure is relaxed, as heard on track 2. Is the note you play like that on the CD? If it is very different you may need to alter your embouchure. Ask your teacher for help with this.

Buzzing exercises should form part of your "warm up" routine each time you play. To help you do this, each stage of *The Boosey Brass Method* trombone book 1 begins with a *Warm-ups* section. Every time you use this book, be sure to practise the *Warm-ups* of the stage that you are working on.

Looking after your instrument

It is important to store your trombone safely in its case. Your trombone will easily dent and this will affect the tuning. Always transport it in its case. Secure your mouthpiece and other accessories as they can come loose and scratch your trombone. Never put anything in the case that will put pressure on your instrument, for example, lots of sheet music.

When you have finished playing, twist the mouthpiece free and replace it in the case. Drain excess moisture away using the water key, return the tuning slide to the closed position and engage the slide lock. Use a soft, clean cloth (a special polishing cloth is best) to remove dust and fingerprints from your trombone. Undo the locking screw and gently separate both parts of your trombone by moving the bell section slightly side to side. Place the instrument firmly in the case and make sure the case is properly closed before lifting it up.

Caring for the slide

The slide is an extremely important part of your trombone so it is essential that it moves smoothly. To clean it, firstly remove the outer slide and lay it somewhere safe. Wipe the inner slide clean using a lint free cloth. Apply a small amount of slide cream (available from most music shops) to the ends of the inner slide and ensure that it is evenly coated with a thin film. Next, use a small spray bottle to spray water over the inner slide. Replace the outer slide and move it in and out to spread the slide cream evenly. Spray a small amount of water onto the slide each time you play.

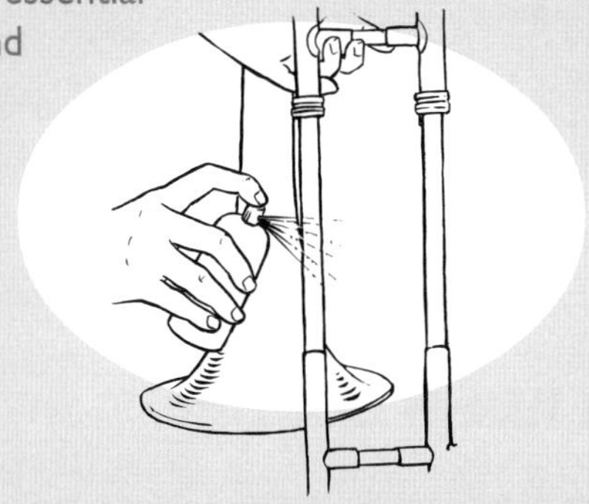

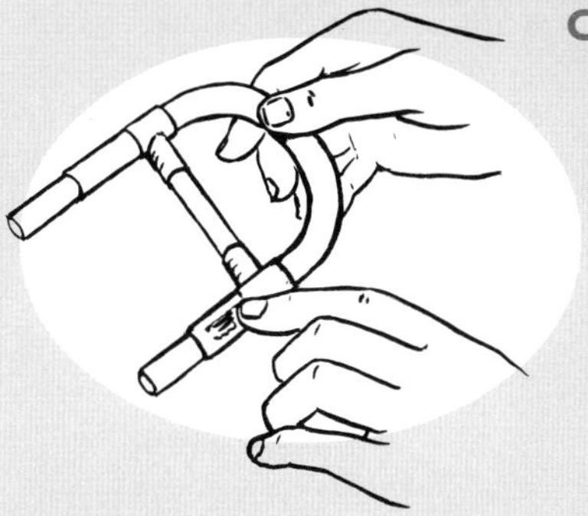

Caring for the tuning slide

The tuning slide is also an important part of your trombone and needs to be cleaned regularly. Remove the slide and clean it with a tissue or a lint-free cloth. Then apply a thin layer of petroleum jelly or specialist slide grease. Replace the slide and move in and out to ensure the tuning slide grease is evenly spread. Remove any excess with a cloth.

Tuning

You may find that your trombone sounds slightly higher or lower than the same note on the CD or other instruments. If it does you will need to adjust it - this is called tuning. You do this by moving the main tuning slide (see page 4) - ask your teacher for help with this.

Tune your trombone to the note **F** (see page 8). Play track 2 of the CD to hear this note then play **F** on your trombone. Listen carefully to both notes. Is your note the same, or is it slightly higher or lower than the CD?

If your note is higher than the tuning note, you will need to pull out the main tuning slide by a tiny amount. If it is lower, gently push the main tuning slide in.

There is no set position for the main tuning slide, and you will find that its position will vary each time you play.

Golden Rules

- Never let your lips or cheeks puff out
- Keep the mouthpiece in the middle of your mouth
- Always touch the mouthpiece lightly against your lips and don't press – it should never leave a dent on your lips
- Always tongue against your teeth, don't let your tongue come through your lips
- Breathe deeply before playing, don't move your shoulders as you breathe in
- Always strive for a good quality sound, don't blow too loudly
- Always moisten your lips before playing

Warm-ups

Always use these exercises to warm up before playing any part of stage 1

See the mouthpiece buzzing exercise on page 6

Using only the mouthpiece, buzz these blocks. Don't forget to use your tongue to start each block (but not to stop each block).

long	rest	long	rest

Now buzz shorter sounds.

shor-	ter	rest	shor-	ter	rest

Then buzz these patterns of long and shorter sounds.

long		rest	shor-	ter	rest
shor-	ter	rest	long		rest

Echo Games

Buzz or clap these *Echo Games* with your teacher:

Make up your own Echo Games too.

	echo		echo
	echo		echo

Playing F

The note **F** is in first position, with the slide fully in. To play **F** ensure that your embouchure is relaxed enough. You can hear **F** on track 2 of the CD, or ask your teacher to play it.

This is what **F** looks like written down.

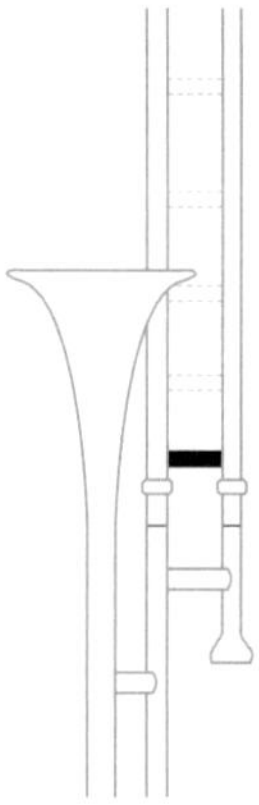

Starting Blocks

Use **F** to play these blocks - slowly at first, then a little faster:

long		rest	shor-	ter	rest
shor-	ter	rest	long		rest

Fanfare Time

Join in with *Fanfare Time* on track 1 of the CD. Here is your part written as blocks. Wait for the opening fanfare to finish, then play your part four times on the note **F**. Take a breath after each long note.

Create your own pattern of long and shorter notes to go with Fanfare Time.

This is what your part for *Fanfare Time* looks like written out as music.

This sign is called a *bass clef*. You will see this at the beginning of each line of trombone music.

Music is written on sets of five lines called a *staff*.

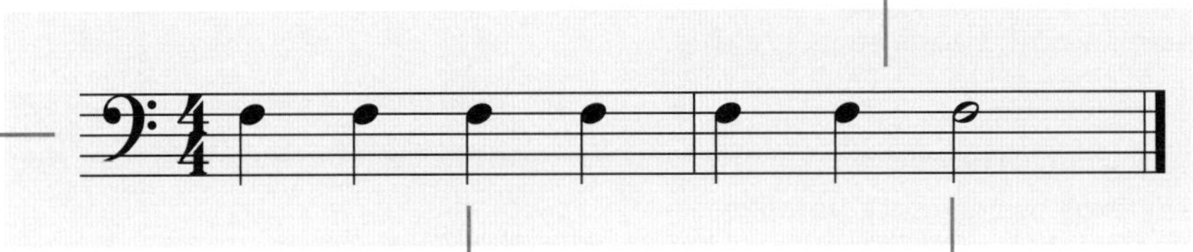

The shorter notes are filled in.

The longer notes are hollow.

One Two Watch

The sound on track 3 is called a **pulse**. A pulse keeps going without changing. It's like the ticking of a watch or clock. Each sound of the pulse is called a **beat**. A pattern of notes of different lengths is called a **rhythm**.

A one-beat note is called a *crotchet* or *quarter note*. It has a filled-in notehead.

A two-beat note is called a *minim* or *half note*. It has a hollow notehead.

There is a pulse in most of the music you have ever listened to, danced to, sung or played.

First, play the rhythm, written as blocks.

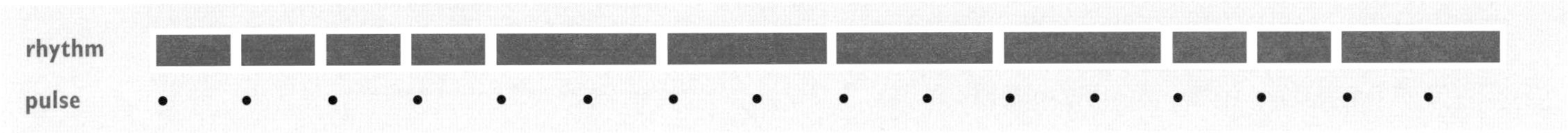

Now play the rhythm again, using the note symbols.

This sign tells you to take a breath.

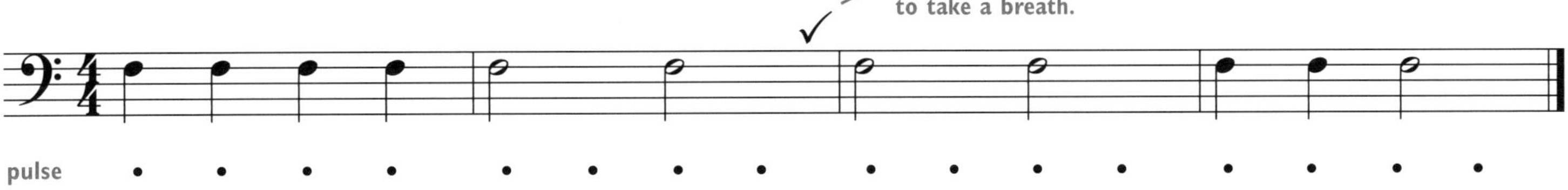

Feeling the Rhythm

You can speak in rhythm, clap, tap your feet, dance - even think in rhythm. Say the words below and clap or step the rhythms with the pulse on track 3 of the CD.

Can you think up some other words to fit with either of the rhythms?

Rhythm Grid

Make up your own piece using long and short notes. Don't forget to give your piece a title

Look at the rhythms in the grid. You can work across, up or down the grid in any order you like. Using the backing on track 4 as an accompaniment, try the following:

- buzz or clap the rhythms
- sing the rhythms on any note you like
- "think" the rhythms in your head
- play the rhythms using **F**

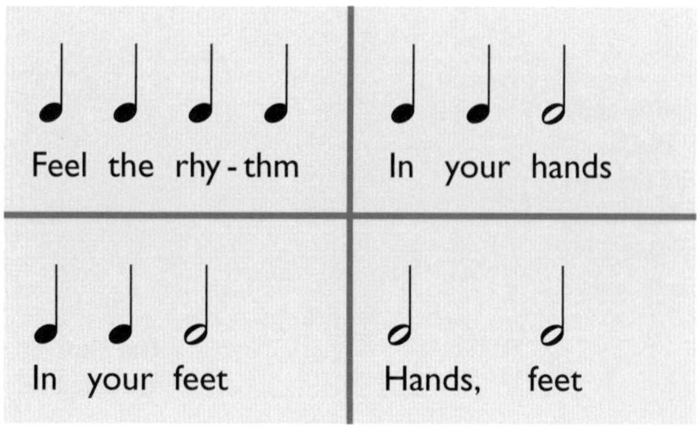

Echo Games

Make up your own Echo Games too.

With your teacher, buzz, clap, sing or play these *Echo Games*:

E-zy to Play

Clap or buzz the rhythm of this tune. Have you clapped it or played it before? Then play it using the note **F**.

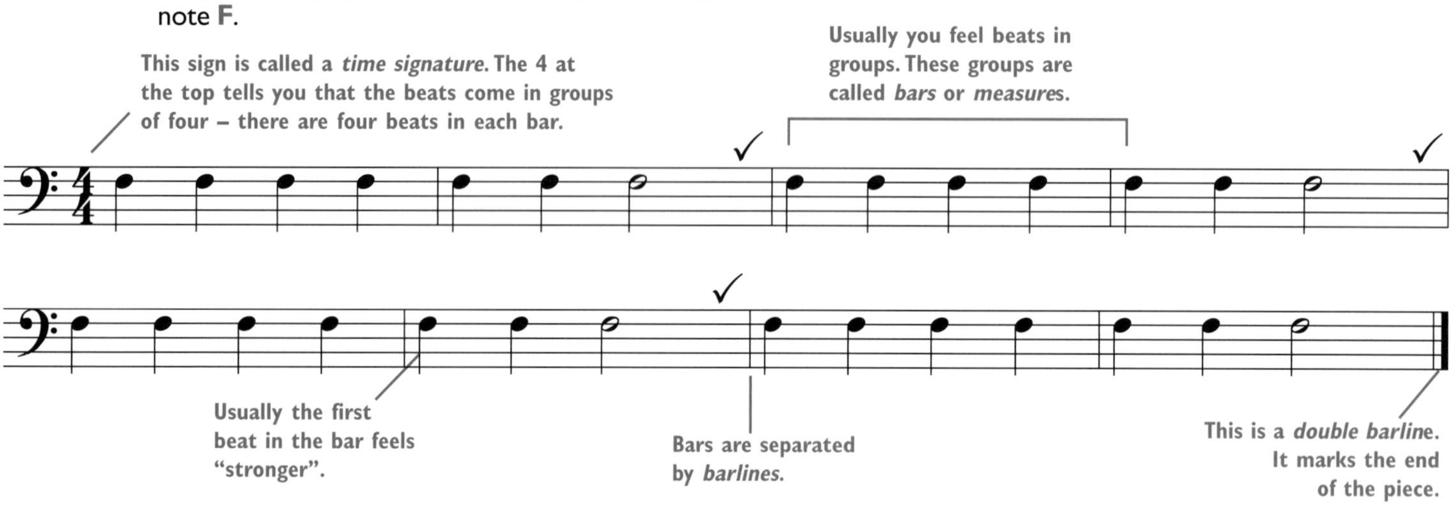

Listen to some of your favourite music and decide how the beats are grouped – in twos, threes, fours?

High Hopes

Use the note **F**. Remember to take a breath where you see the sign.

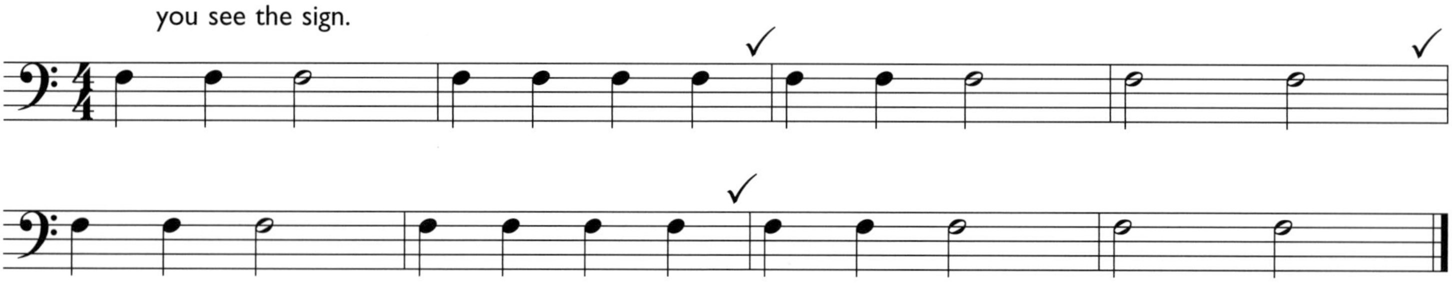

Feeling the Rhythm

Count or step the pulse and clap the rhythm.
Turn your palms upwards for each rest.

This sign is a two-beat rest. It tells you not to play for two beats.

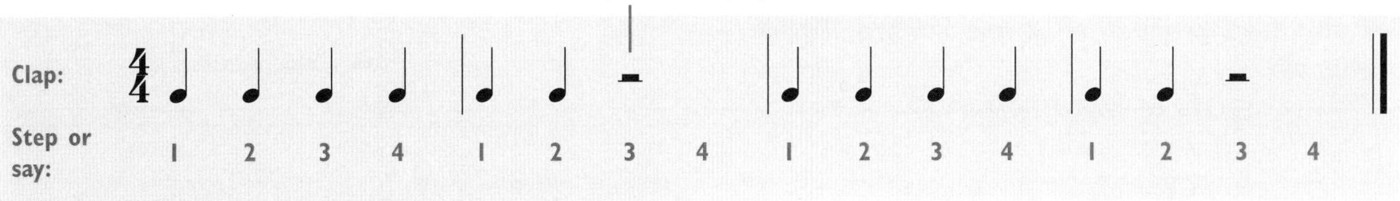

On the Spot

Listen to track 7 on the CD and count with the pulse which you can hear in the low notes of the piano part.

Then play *On the Spot* using the note **F**. During the rests, count the beat carefully and take a breath.

This sign is a whole-bar rest. It tells you not to play for a whole bar.

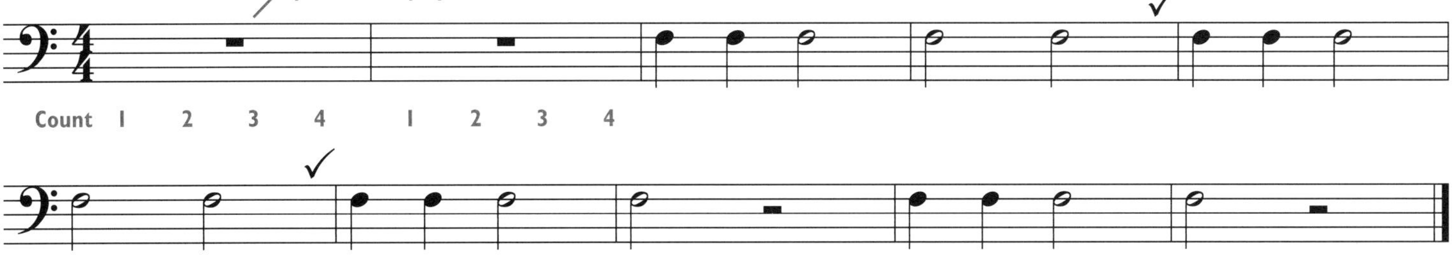

In and Out

You don't need to use your instrument for *In and Out*. You can do this anywhere - going to school, in the bath, watching TV.

Breathe in				**Breathe out**			
count				*count*			
1	**2**	**3**	**4**	**1**	**2**	**3**	**4**

Go! Stop!

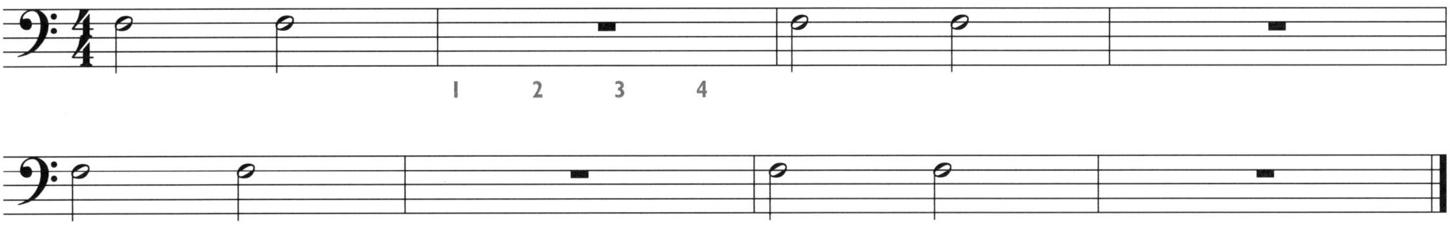

You can play *Go! Stop!* using other rhythms too.
Instead of 𝅗𝅥 𝅗𝅥 try one of the rhythms on the right:

High and low

Sing a high note followed by a low note, then a low note followed by a high note. **Pitch** is the word for how high or low a note is.

Using your mouthpiece only, buzz a higher sound and a lower sound. In order to play a higher buzz, gently tighten or 'firm' your embouchure very slightly to make your lips vibrate faster. You will also need to provide faster air support. Ask your teacher for help.

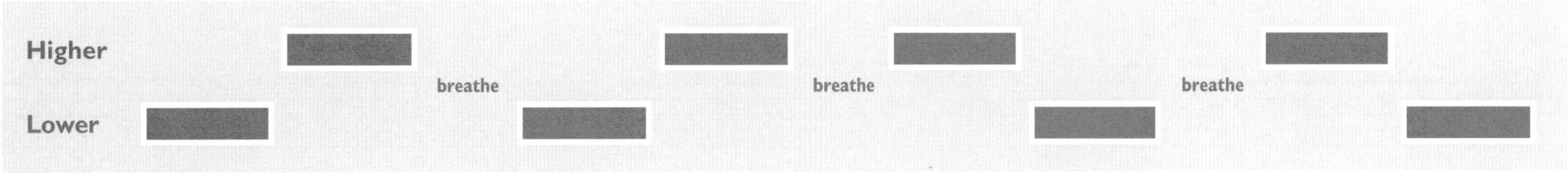

Playing E flat

Have you warmed up properly? Go to page 8.

To play the note E♭, extend the slide to third position. The slide support is roughly opposite the bell end. E♭ is lower in pitch than F, therefore you will also need to slightly relax your lips and provide slower air.

This is what E♭ looks like written down:

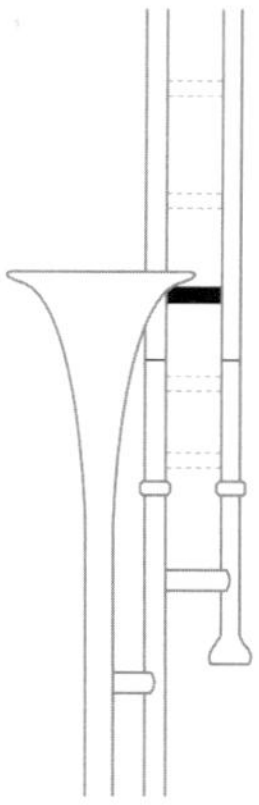

More about flats

The flat sign lowers a note by a small step known as a semitone. ♭

Building Blocks

Use E♭ and F to play these blocks – slowly at first, then a little faster:

Try these Building Blocks with a metronome or with track 4

Echo Games

With your teacher, buzz the rhythm, clap, sing or play these *Echo Games*.

Make up your own Echo Games too.

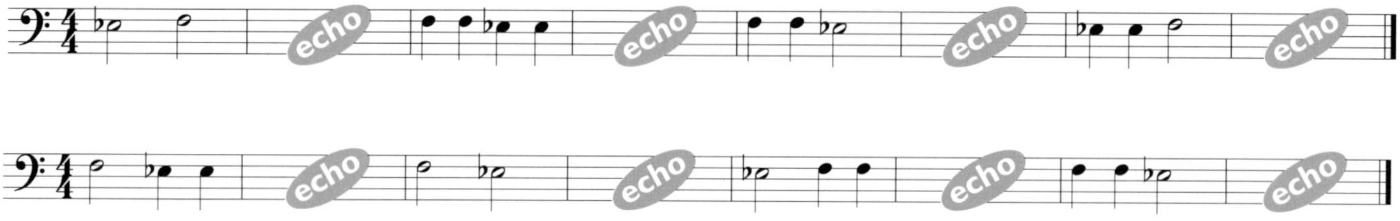

Another Way

A flat sign lasts until the next barline.
So this flat applies to both Es.

Thinking Time

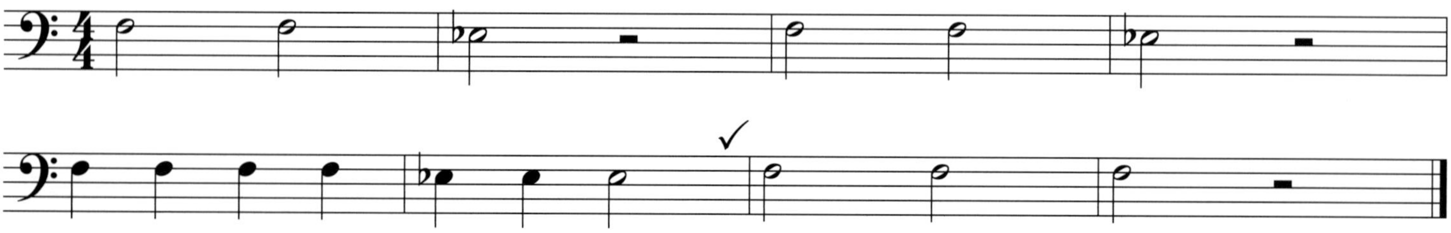

Learning a new piece

CLAP - Decide a speed for the pulse, count a few bars, then clap the rhythm of the piece to the pulse.

SING - Sing the tune to the note names.

THINK - "Think" the piece - that means put the slide in the position of the notes and think the tune in your head, but don't blow your trombone yet.

PLAY - Count the pulse, take a breath, then play.

Summer Song

Clap, sing, think, then play.

Did the piece sound the way you imagined it? If not, what were the differences?

Moving On

Now play *Moving On* again, this time using any of the rhythms in the grid in any order.

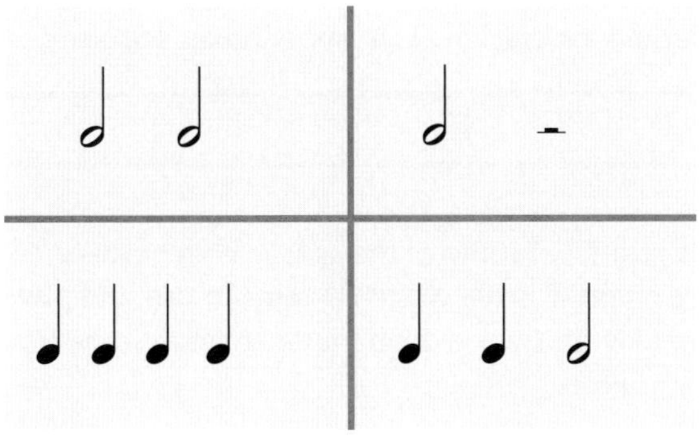

Play the first four bars of Another Way from memory.

Here on my Own

There are two versions of *Here on my Own* on the CD. What are the differences? Which do you prefer? Clap, sing, think, then play.

The sign above this note is called a *pause*. It tells you to hold the note for a little longer than usual.

Playing G

Have you warmed up properly? Go to page 8.

To play the note **G**, extend the slide to fourth position. The end of the outer slide is roughly opposite the bell end. You will need to slightly firm your lips and provide faster air. This is what **G** looks like written down:

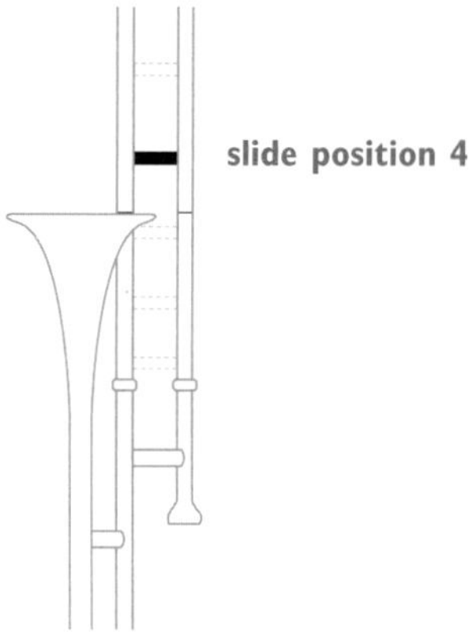

Building Blocks

Using **E♭**, **F** and **G** play these blocks slowly, then a little faster.

Try these Building Blocks with a metronome or with track 4

Echo Games

With your teacher, buzz, clap, sing or play the following *Echo Games*.

Make up your own Echo Games too.

Note Grid

Each box represents one bar of 4/4. Decide which rhythms to use from the grid on the right and play with the backing on track 4. The empty boxes are rests.

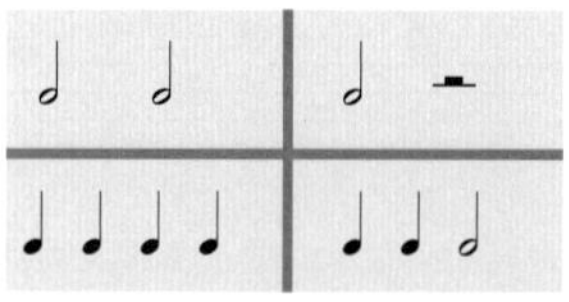

E♭	E♭	F		F	G	E♭	

In this grid, fill in some of the spaces with notes and leave others empty. Decide which rhythms to use, and play with the backing on track 4. Remember to leave some boxes empty as rests.

Mole Hill

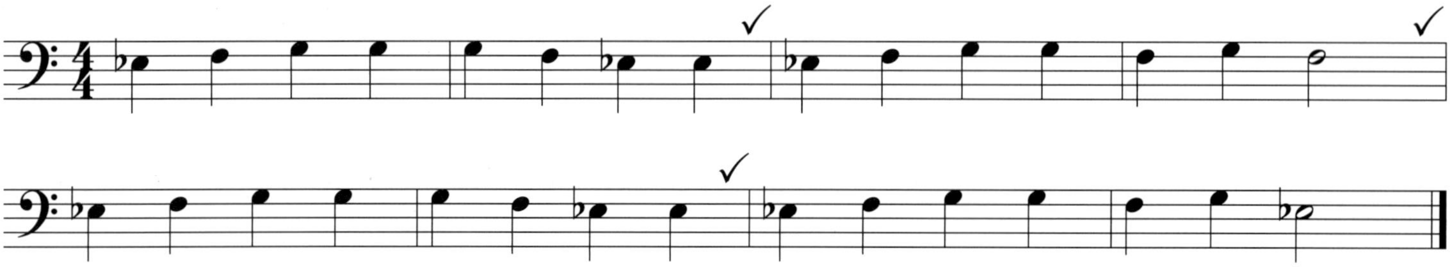

Au clair de la lune

This is a French folk song. Its title means "by the light of the moon".

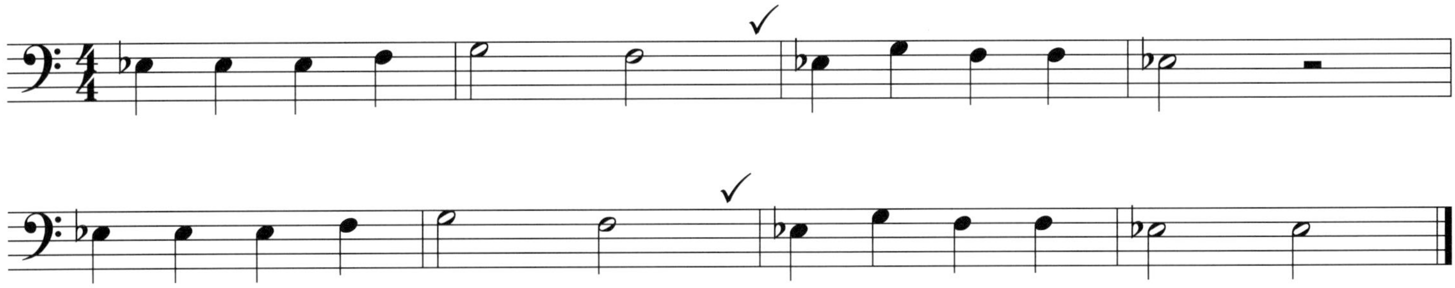

Shore to Sea

Zoom in on the shaded bar. Use the practice hints on the right.

- Play the shaded area slowly.
- Put the slide into the position for each note and imagine how they will sound.
- Play them with your eyes closed.

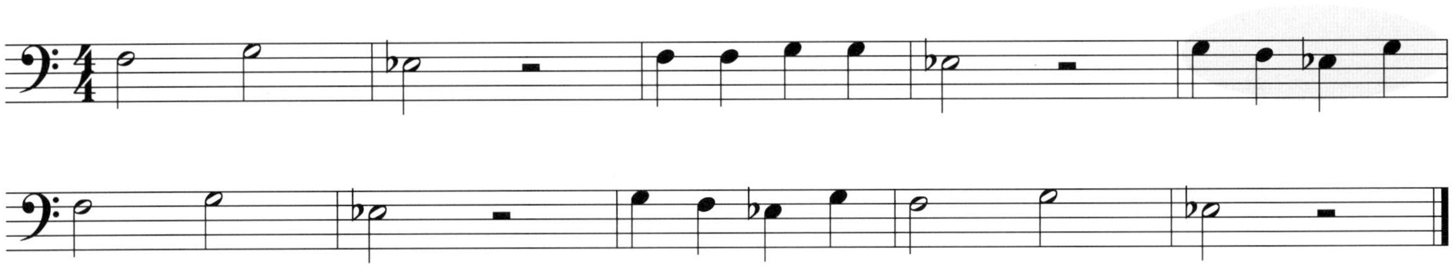

Together

This piece is for you and your teacher. A piece for two players is called a **duet**. Use the practice hints on the right to help you get ready to play it.

- Play your part for the other player, then ask them to play their part for you. Listen carefully!
- Before you start to play, count the pulse together for at least two bars.
- While you are playing, listen to the other person as well as to yourself!

Questions and Answers

Using E♭, F and G, make up your own "answers" to these "questions". You could include a pattern of notes or a rhythm that you hear in the question.

Play the first four bars of Moving on *(page 13) from memory.*

- Clap, buzz or play an answer on one note.

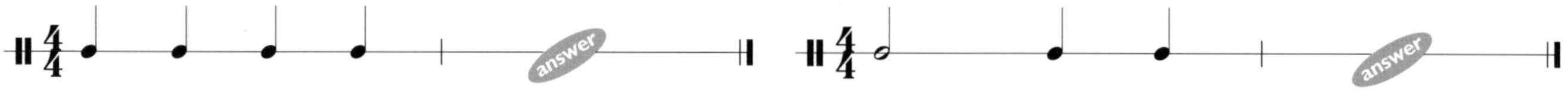

- Play an answer using any notes you know.

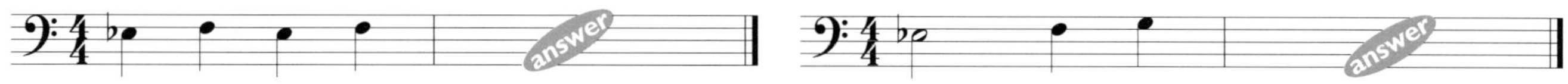

Half-beat notes

Half-beat notes are called **quavers** or **eighth notes**. Two or more quavers together are linked together by a line called a **beam**.

A single quaver has a tail.

Groups of quavers are joined together by beams.

Feeling the Rhythm

Count a pulse or use track 4 on the CD. Step the rhythms below. During the rests, count silently.

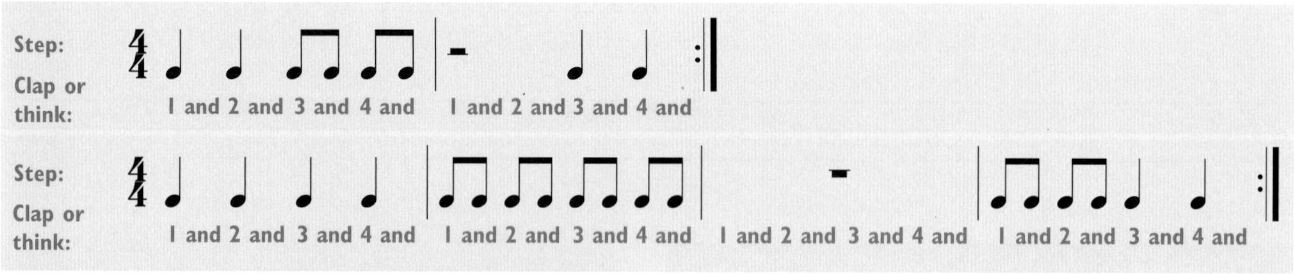

Dolphin Club

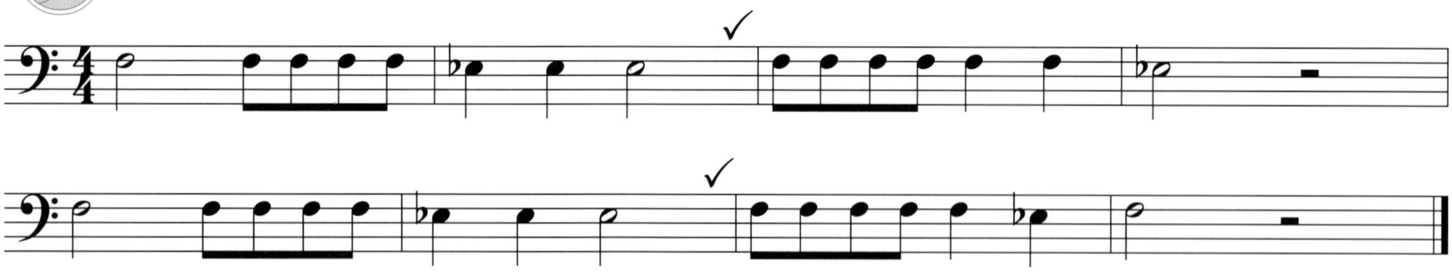

Beguine

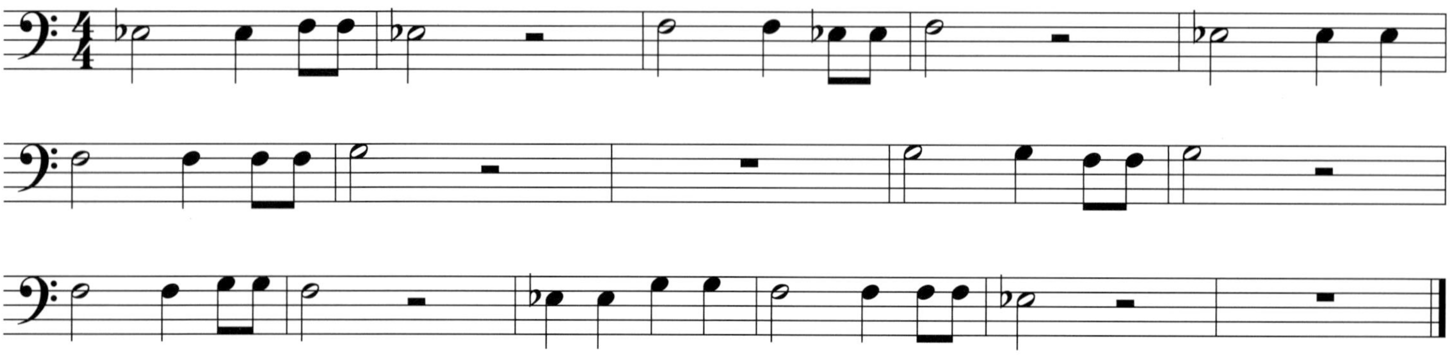

Warm-ups

Buzz two different sounds firstly without your mouthpiece, then with your mouthpiece only:

Buzz the following rhythm – slowly, then a little faster:

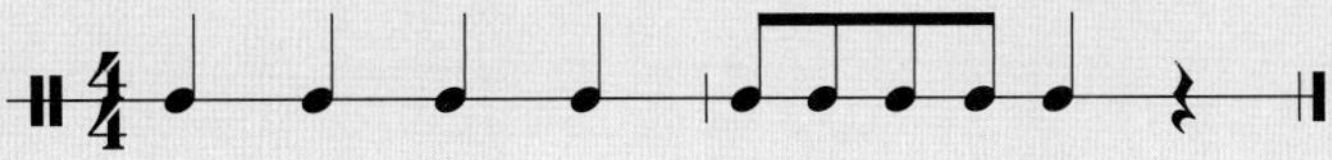

Now play these blocks:

Always use these exercises to warm up before playing any part of Stage 2

Playing D

To play the note **D**, extend the slide to 4th position. Avoid touching the bell for 4th position. To play **D**, and to avoid playing **G**, you will need to relax your lips slightly and provide slower air.

This is what **D** looks like written down.

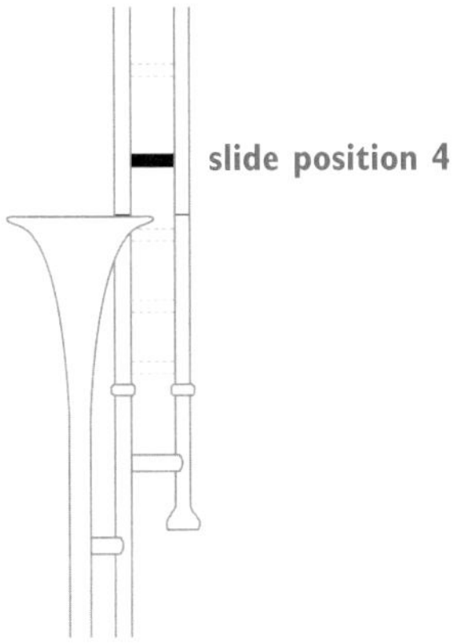

Building Blocks

Using **D**, **E♭** and **F** play these blocks slowly, then a little faster.

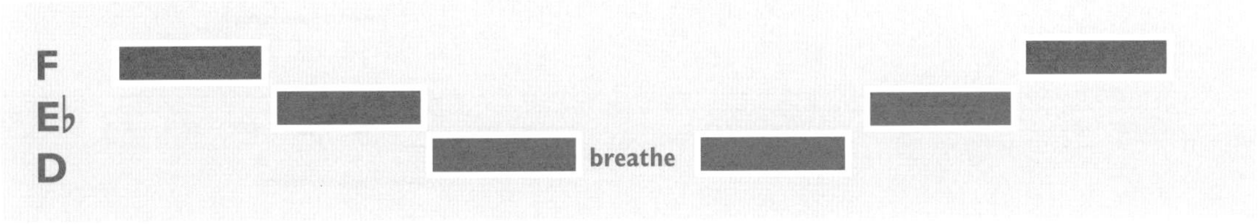

Try these building blocks with a metronome or track 4.

Echo Games

With your teacher, buzz, clap, sing or play these *Echo Games*.

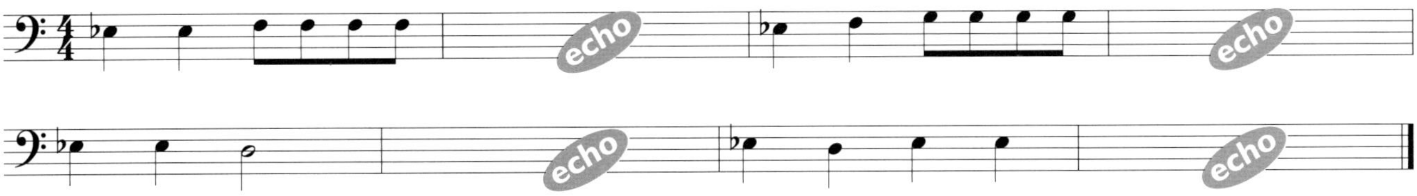

Make up your own Echo Games too.

Down in the Dumps

Chris Morgan

19 Looking Back

Chris Morgan

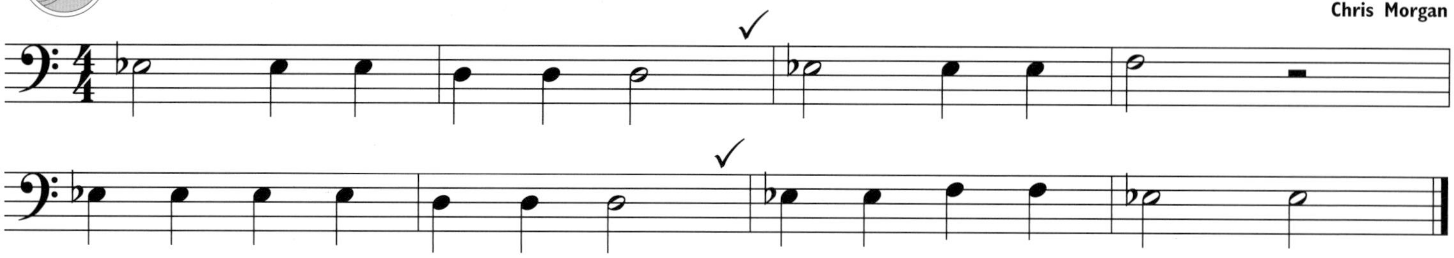

Questions and Answers

Using **D**, **E♭**, **F** and **G** make up your own "answers" to these "questions". You could include a pattern of notes or a rhythm that you hear in the question.

- Clap an answer or play an answer on one note.

- Play an answer using any notes you know. You could use the starting and finishing notes shown.

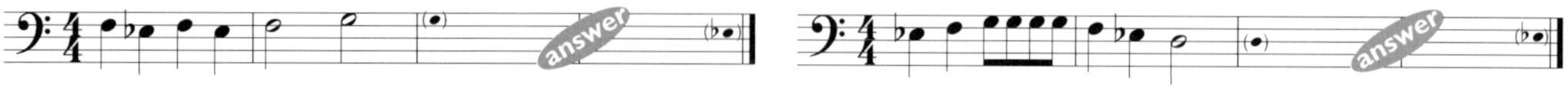

20 Awesome

Zoom in on the shaded bars, using the practice hints on page 15.

Chris Morgan

These two dots are a *repeat sign*. They mean "go back to the start and play the piece again".

Do it Yourself!

Make your own rhythm. Start to clap or buzz some rhythms, trying lots of different ideas. When you find one you like, write it down.

Play the first two bars of *Awesome*. Do the notes move by step, or are there jumps? Now play the first two bars of *Down in the Dumps*. Steps or jumps?

Invent two pieces using your rhythm, and the notes **D**, **E♭**, **F** and **G**. Start and end on the notes shown. Again, try lots of different ideas.

Start your first piece with notes that move by step:

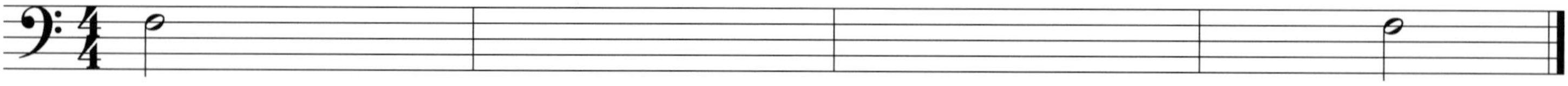

Start your second piece with a jump:

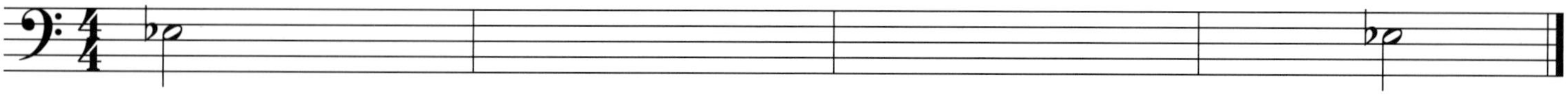

A new time signature

The 2 at the top of this time signature tells you that there are two beats in each bar.

2/4

The 4 underneath tells you that the beats are crotchets or quarter notes.

Feeling the Rhythm

Set up a regular 2/4 pulse, by counting "1, 2, 1, 2" out loud. Then clap or buzz the rhythm.

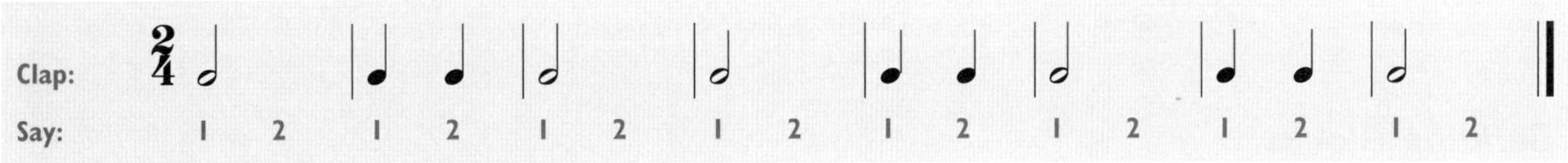

Play the rhythm above, using any note. Then make up your own tune using some of the notes you have learned. You could ask a friend to set up a 2/4 pulse with a percussion instrument.

Little March

Chris Morgan

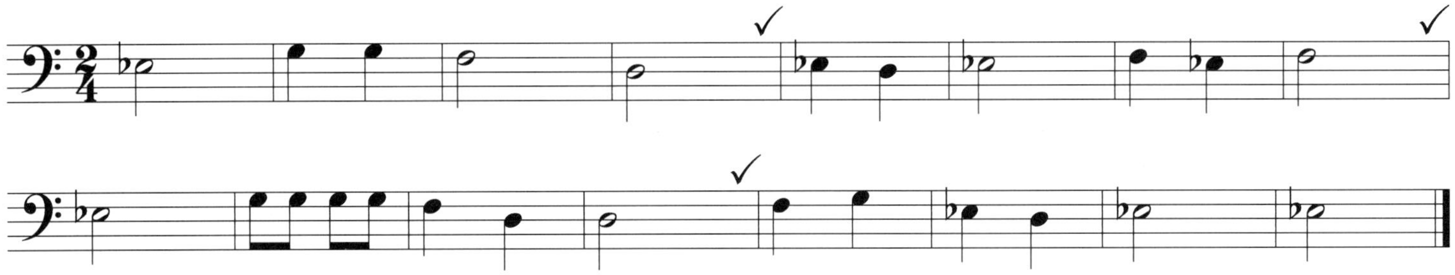

Again and Again

This piece has a repeated pattern of notes. How many times does it appear? Can you play the piece without looking at the music?

Chris Morgan

Playing B♭

To play the note **B♭**, the slide should be in first position (fully in). To play **B♭**, and to avoid playing **F**, ensure your embouchure is relaxed enough. To hear **B♭** listen to track 22.

This is what **B♭** looks like written down:

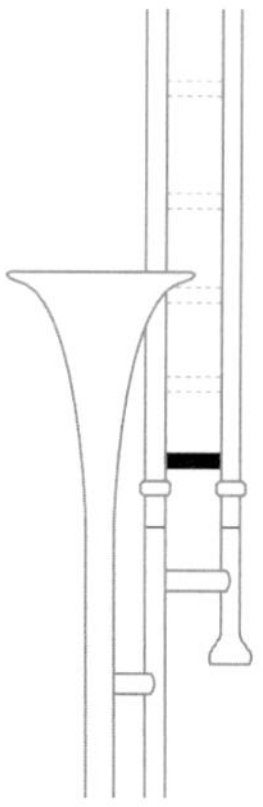

Building Blocks

Using **B♭**, **D**, **E♭** and **F** play these blocks slowly, then a little faster.

Try these Building Blocks with a metronome or with track 4

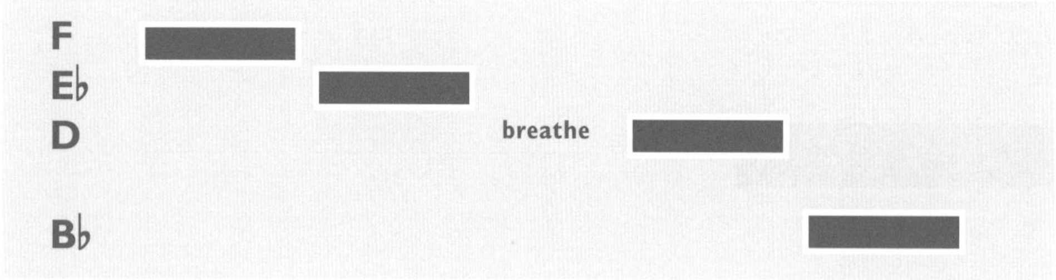

Echo Games

With your teacher, buzz the rhythm, clap, sing or play these *Echo Games*.

Up and Down

Play the notes below with the backing on track 23. Count carefully!

Chris Morgan

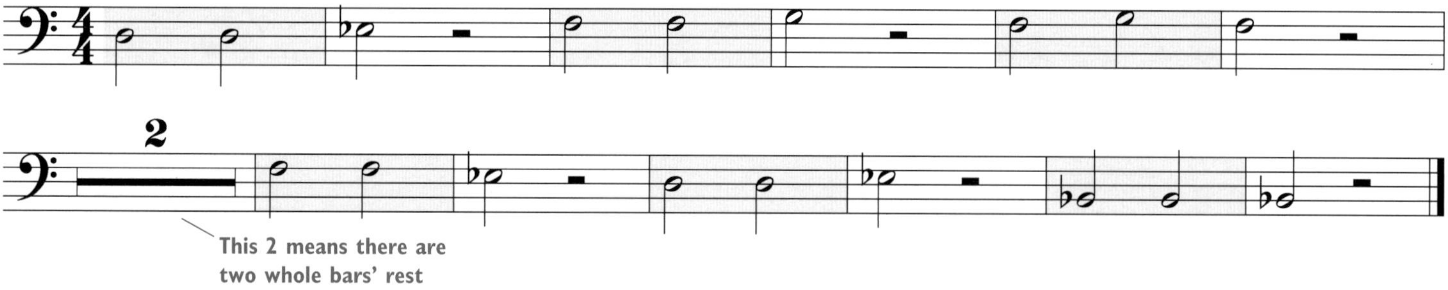

You can play *Up and Down* using other rhythms too. Try one of the rhythms from the grid in the highlighted bars:

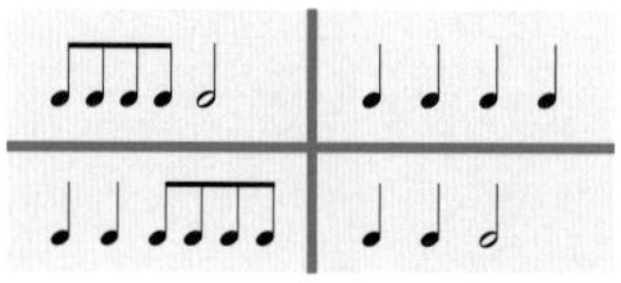

Feeling the Rhythm

Use track 4 of the CD to keep a pulse while you clap this rhythm twice. Turn your palms upwards when you get to the rests.

This sign is a *crotchet rest* or *quarter rest*. It lasts for one beat.

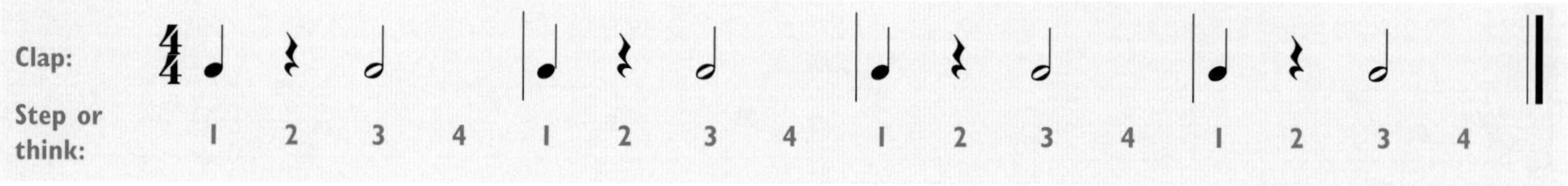

Step the pulse while you say these words to the rhythm.

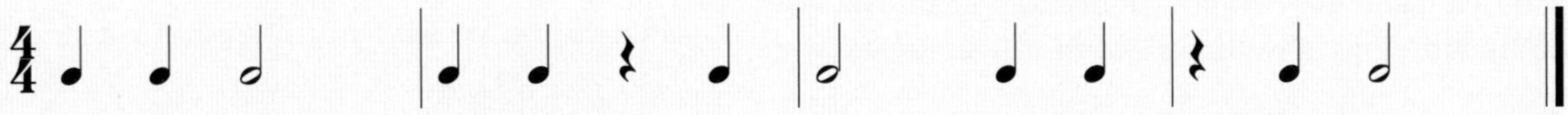

Say: I will take — one short (rest) and then — I will (rest) a - gain —.

Step: 1 2 3 4 1 2 3 4 1 2 3 4 1 2 3 4

Whisper or "think" the word "rest".

Beach Hut

You can play *Beach Hut* as a duet, with the CD, or with anyone using a *Boosey Woodwind* or *Boosey Brass* book.

Sharps or flats at the beginning of a line of music are called the *key signature*. This one tells you to play B♭ every time you see the note B and E♭ when you see the note E.

Chris Norton

A new time signature

The 3 at the top of this time signature means that there are three beats in each bar.

3/4

Feeling the Rhythm

Do these activities with the pulse on track 25 of the CD.

Say: Too ta ta Too ta ta Too ta ta Too ta ta

Think: 1 2 3 1 2 3 1 2 3 1 2 3

Sway: right left right left

Fanfare Time

Listen to track 26 on the CD and join in on the after the fanfare. This time the piece has three beats in a bar.

Listen to the version of Fanfare Time on track 26 and then to the version you played in stage 1 (track 2). Can you feel the difference in the rhythm?

Play this four times:

This note is called a *dotted minim* or *dotted half note.* Hold it for 3 beats.

In and Out

This time, count three beats for each breath.

Breathe in			Breathe out			Breathe in			Breathe out		
count			count			count			count		
1	2	3	1	2	3	1	2	3	1	2	3

Note Grid

Each box represents one bar of 3/4. Decide on which rhythms to use from the grid on the right and play with the backing on track 25. The empty boxes are rests.

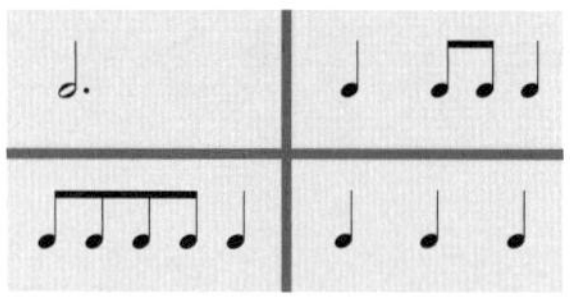

E♭	G	F		F	E♭	D	E♭

Can you make your own note grid using the rhythms above and any notes you know? Remember to leave some boxes empty as rests.

Echo Games

With your teacher, buzz, clap, sing or play these *Echo Games.*

City Streets

There are two versions of this piece on the CD. What are the differences? Which do you prefer?

Chris Norton

Icelandic Lullaby

29

traditional

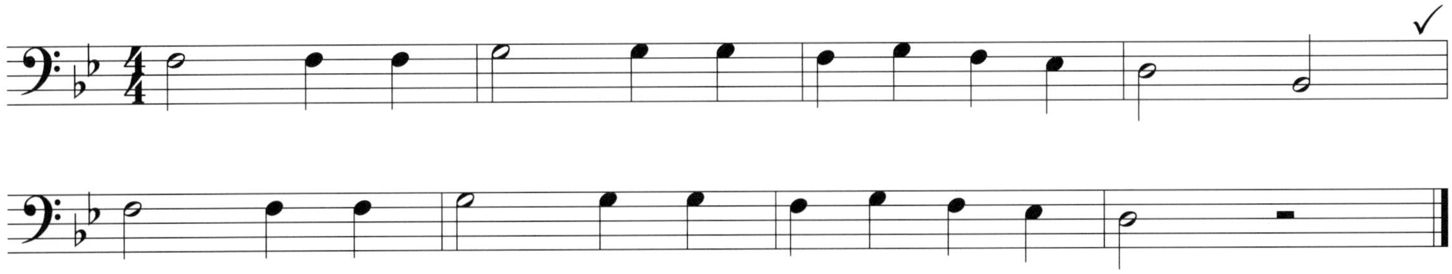

Pacing

30

Chris Norton

Note Ladders

Choose one rhythm pattern from the rhythm grid and use it to play each note in the note ladders. Move up and down the ladders by step.

Clap your rhythm first, then sing the notes of the ladders. Next, "think" notes and the rhythm. Finally, play your ladders.

Then choose another rhythm. Again, clap, sing, think and play the ladders.

Climb up from here...

Joining notes together

A curved line joining different notes is called a **slur**. It tells you to move between the notes smoothly.

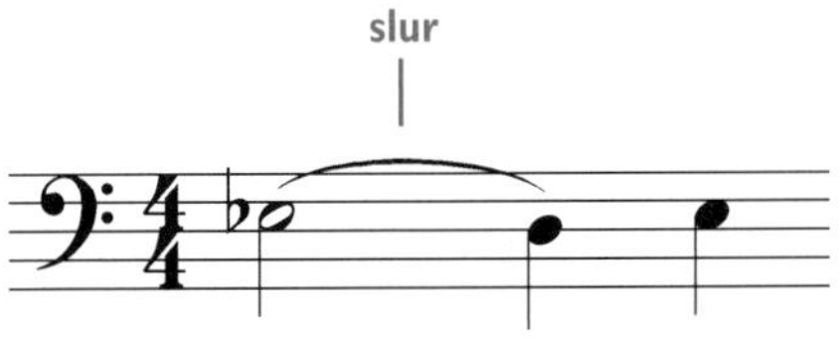

Smooth Moves

31

Zoom in on the shaded bar. To move smoothly between E♭ and D, tongue the first note normally and **soft tongue** (loo or roo) the second.

Chris Morgan

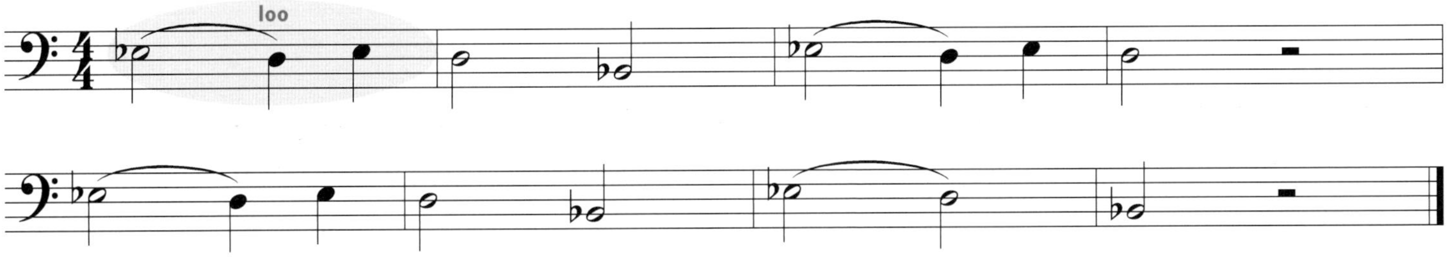

Warm-ups

Buzz two different sounds firstly without your mouthpiece, then with your mouthpiece only:

Always use these exercises to warm up before playing any part of Stage 3

Buzz the following rhythm – slowly, then a little faster:

Now play these blocks:

Echo Games

With your teacher, buzz, clap, sing or play these *Echo Games*.

Make up your own Echo Games too.

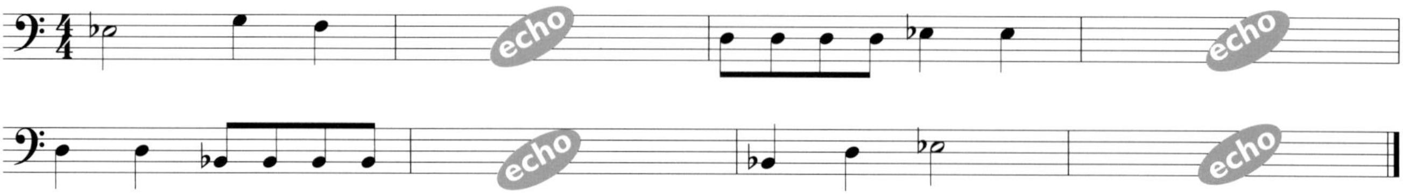

High Jumps

Play these quite slowly.

- Tongue each note.
- When you have played them forwards, start at the end and play the notes in reverse order.

What happens to the size of the jump as you move along the line?

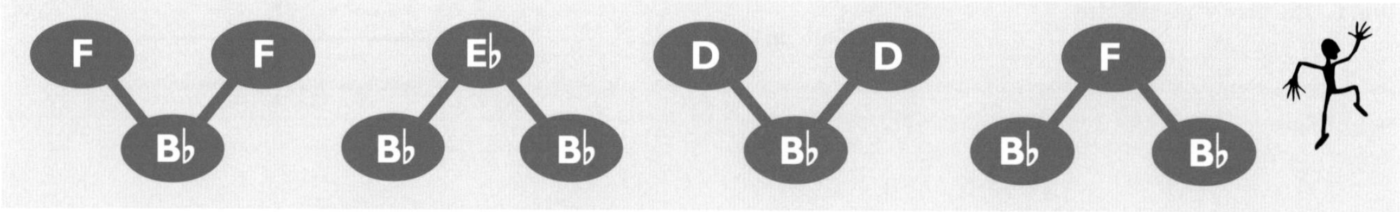

Lazy Days

Zoom in on the shaded bar. You don't need to soft tongue E♭ when slurring from G.

Ian Green

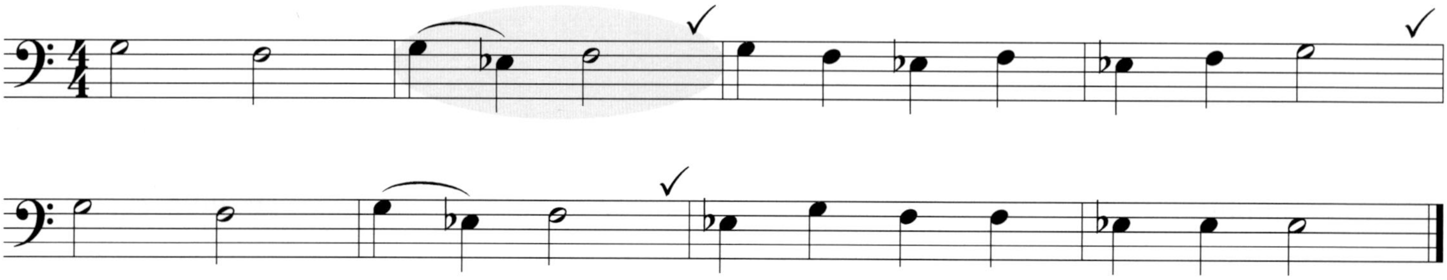

Forest Walk

Ian Green

Four-beat notes

A four-beat note is called a **semibreve** or **whole note**.

A four-beat note has a notehead but no stem.

Sad Times

Zoom in on the shaded bars. You need to soft tongue (loo or roo) E♭ when slurring from F.

Chris Morgan

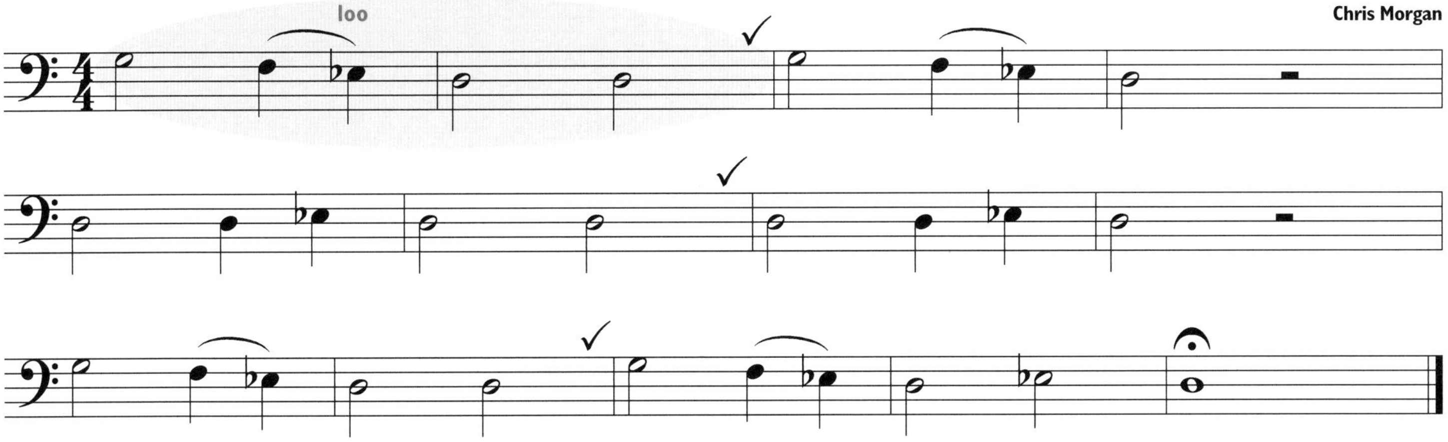

Note Grid

Each box represents one bar of 2/4. Decide on which rhythms to use from the grid on the right and play with the backing on track 33. The empty boxes are rests.

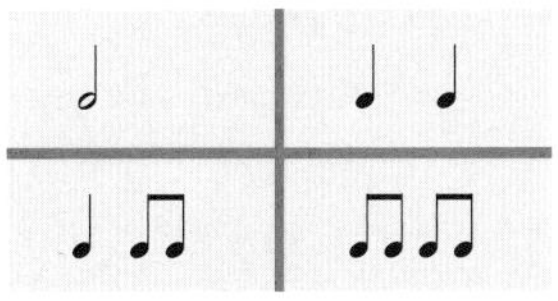

D	B♭	E♭		E♭	F		B♭

Can you make your own note grid using the rhythms above and any notes you know? Remember to leave some boxes empty as rests.

Still Waiting

Zoom in on the shaded bars.

Chris Morgan

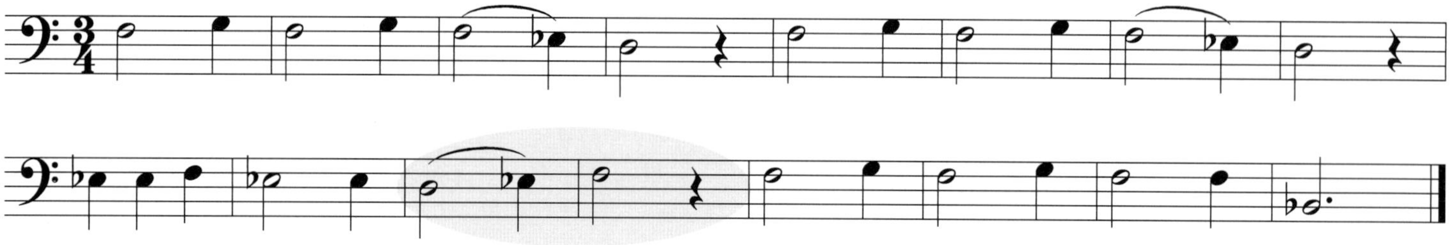

In and Out

Practise the following exercise before playing *Calm Sea.*

Breathe in		**Breathe out**					
count		count					
1	2	3	1	2	3	1	2

Calm Sea

Watch out for the upbeat or anacrusis (say "ana-croo-sis"). There are two versions of this piece on the CD. What are the differences? Which do you prefer?

Chris Morgan

Questions and Answers

Using **B♭**, **D**, **E♭**, **F** and **G** make up your own "answers" to these "questions". You could include a pattern of notes or a rhythm that you hear in the question.

- Clap or buzz an answer or play an answer on one note.

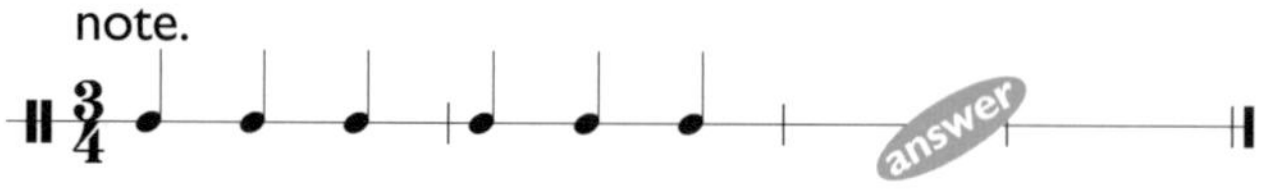

- Play an answer using any notes you know. You could use the starting and finishing notes shown.

Bicycle Ride

Ian Green

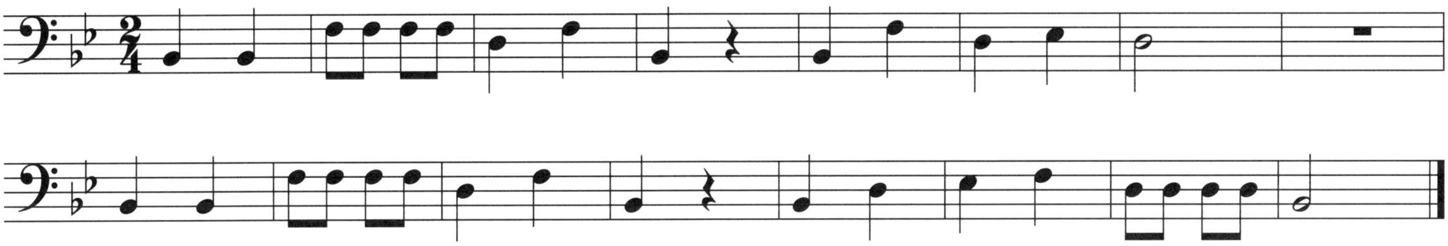

Note Grid

Each box represents one bar of 3/4. Decide on which rhythms to use from the grid on the right and play to the backing on track 25. The empty box is a rest.

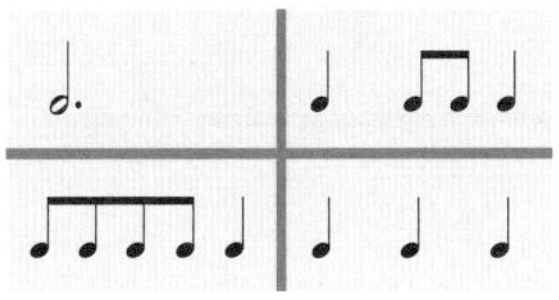

E♭	G	F		F	D		E♭

Can you make your own note grid using the rhythms on the right and any notes you know? Remember to leave some boxes empty as rests.

Try recording your melodies.

Call to Attention

Watch out for the repeat in this piece. When you come to the :‖ sign, repeat back to ‖:

Chris Morgan

Do it Yourself!

Find the tunes you wrote in the *Do it Yourself!* activity on page 18, and play them again a few times. Write them down again, but using **B♭**, **D**, **E♭** and **F** instead.

Play and sing the new versions of your tunes. They will sound quite different.

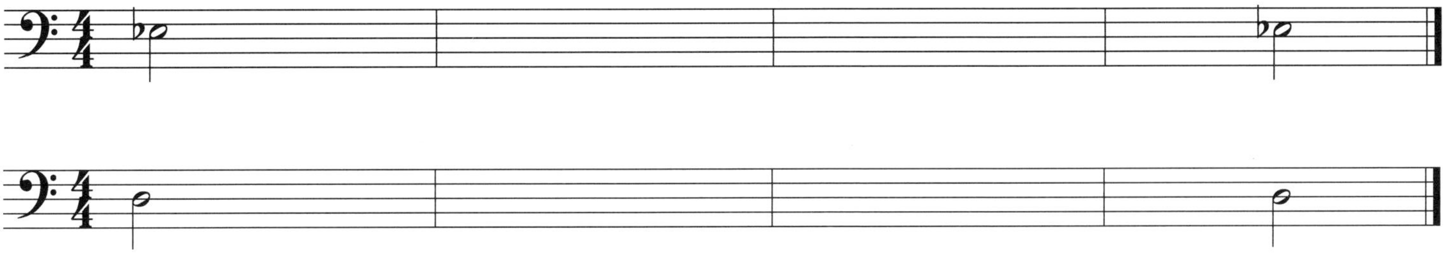

Miles to Go

You can play *Miles to Go* as a duet, with the CD, or with anyone using a *Boosey Woodwind* or *Boosey Brass* book.

Chris Norton

4/4 Rhythm Grid

Play the Rhythm Grid with a drum pattern on a keyboard

Buzz, clap, sing or play up, down or across the grid using the backing on track 4. When you sing or play, use the notes **B**, **D**, **E♭**, **F** and **G**. Don't use more than two notes for any one box.

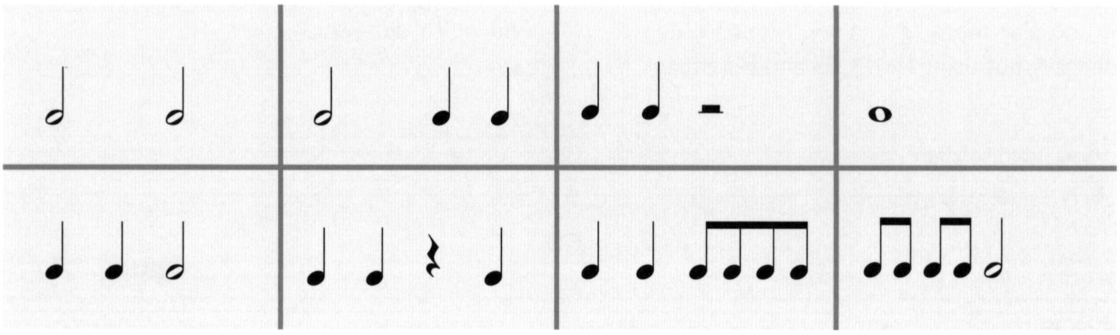

Try recording your melodies

Warm-ups

Buzz two different sounds firstly without your mouthpiece, then with your mouthpiece only:

Always use these exercises to warm up before playing any part of Stage 4

With your mouthpiece only, buzz the following rhythm slowly, then a little faster:

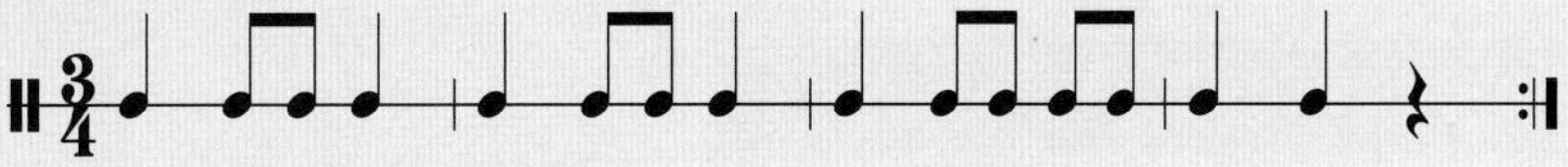

Now play these *High Jumps* quite slowly.

- Tongue each note.
- Slur each group of notes.

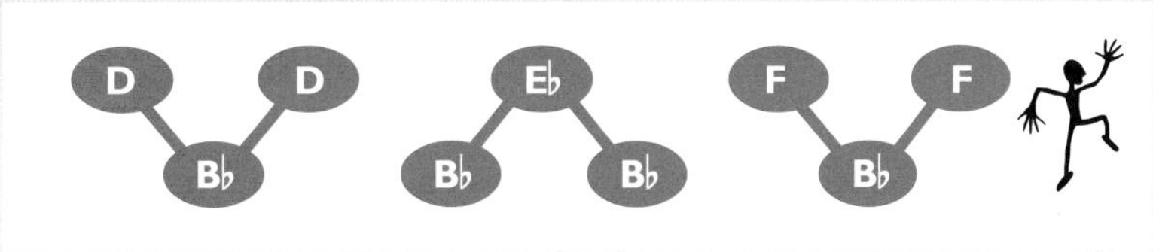

Playing C

To play the note **C**, extend the slide out almost fully into sixth position. Your embouchure and air support should be similar to when you play **low B♭**.

This is what **C** looks like written down:

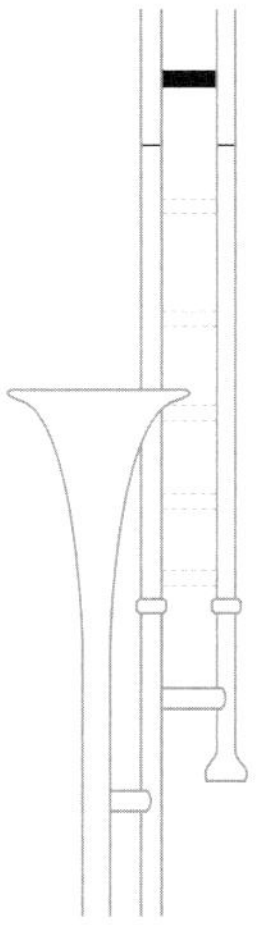

Building Blocks

Using **C**, **D**, **E♭** and **F** play these blocks slowly, then a little faster.

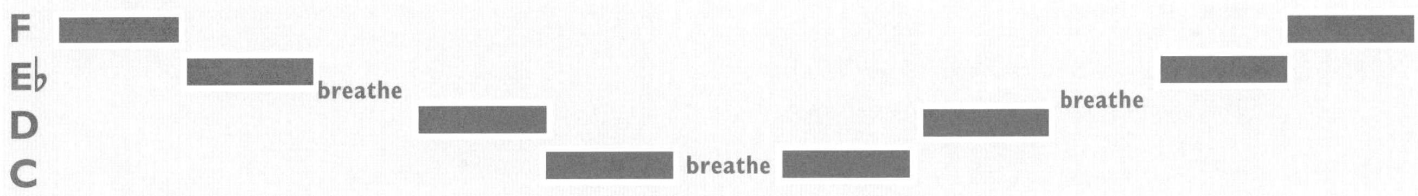

Try these building blocks with a metronome or with track 4

Echo Games

With your teacher, buzz, clap, sing or play these *Echo Games.*

Make up your own Echo Games too.

39 Cactus Tree

Chris Norton

40 Woogie Boogie

Boogie is a jazz dance style which is often played on the piano. Play *Woogie Boogie* with the drum pattern on the right or with a drum pattern on an electronic keyboard. Experiment with the different styles to see which works best.

Play this 9 times:

high drum

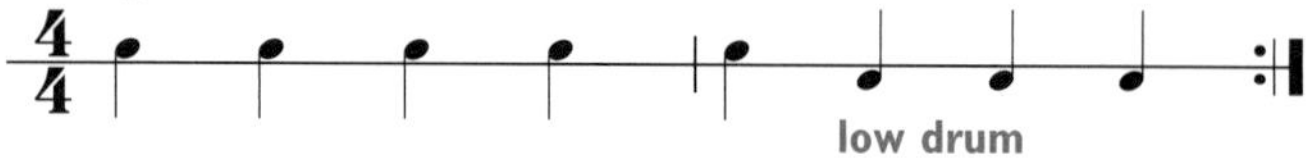

low drum

Anthony Marks

Questions and Answers

Using **B♭**, **C**, **D**, **E♭** and **F**, make up your own "answers" to these "questions". You could include a pattern of notes or a rhythm that you hear in the question.

- Clap an answer or play an answer on one note.

- Play an answer using any notes you know. You could use the starting and finishing notes shown.

41 Now the Day is Over

traditional

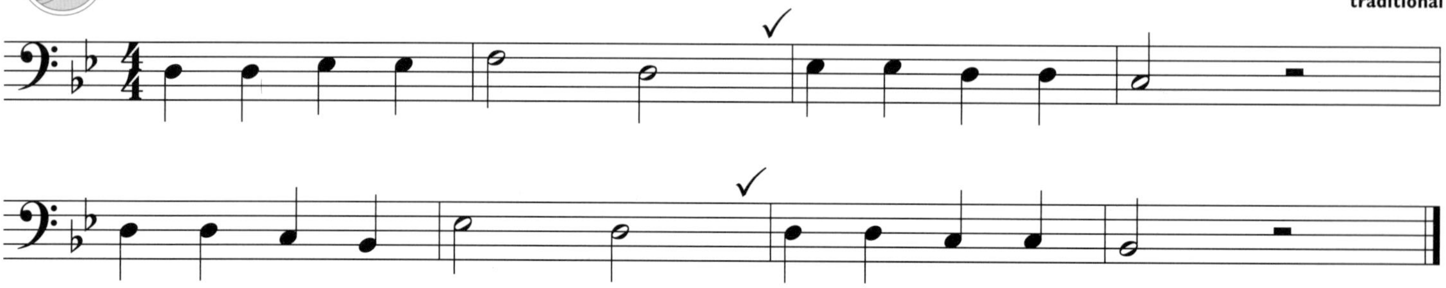

Bird Food

You can play *Bird Food* as a duet, with the CD, or with anyone using a *Boosey Woodwind* or *Boosey Brass* book.

Chris Norton

Mattachins

Mattachins is a sword dance. Learn to play both parts of the duet.

Optional percussion part (play 10 times):

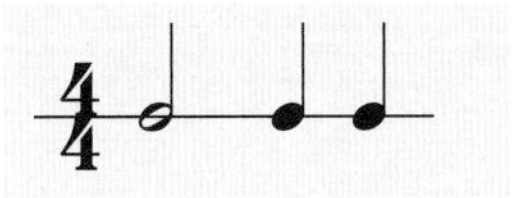

traditional French

Playing low A

To play **low A**, extend the slide into second position. You will also need to relax your embouchure and provide plenty of slow air.

This is what **low A** looks like written down:

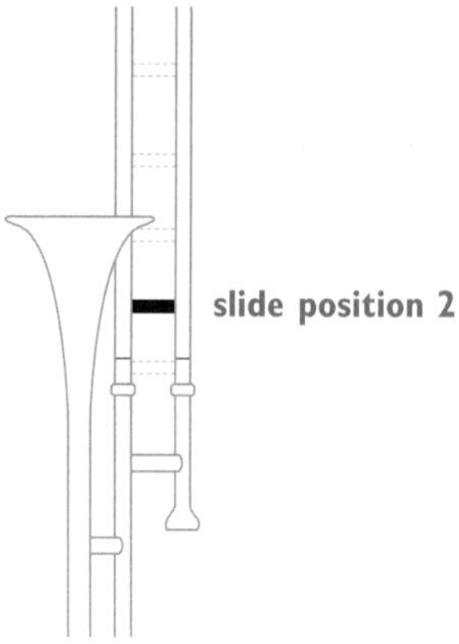

Building Blocks

Using **low A**, **B♭**, **C** and **D** play these blocks slowly, then a little faster.

Try these building blocks with a metronome or with track 4

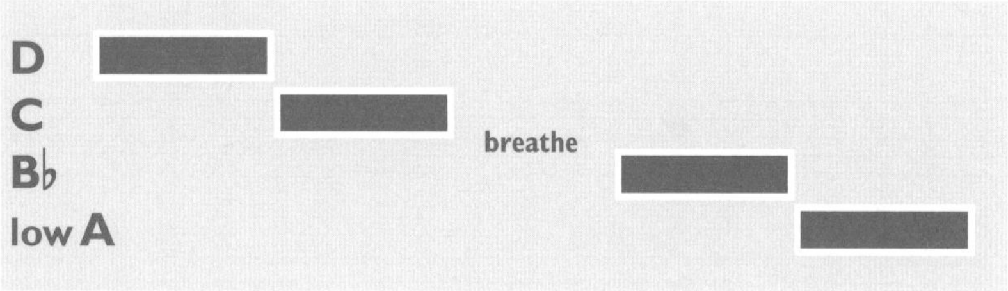

Echo Games

With your teacher, buzz, clap, sing or play these *Echo Games*.

Make up your own Echo Games too.

La Morisque

Tielman Susato

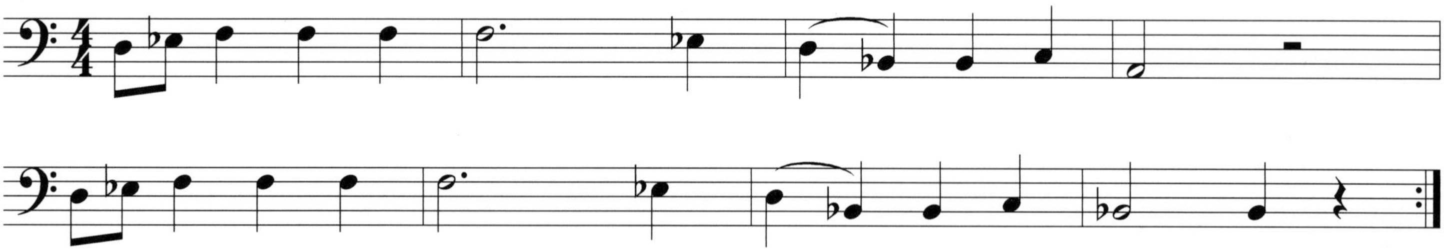

Orangutan Rag

Chris Morgan

Go back to the beginning and play until you reach FINE

Lightly Row

Zoom in on the shaded bars. When you can play this piece, learn to play it from memory by using these practice hints.

- Find any repeated sections
- Sing the tune in your head
- Play short sections without looking at the music

Then play the whole tune from memory.

traditional German

Fast and slow

The speed of a piece is called its **tempo**. Many pieces have words at the beginning to tell you how quickly to play them. These are called **tempo markings**.

Sometimes the words can describe the style or mood of a piece.

Choose a piece you have already learned and play it twice, at two different speeds. Each time, count the pulse before you start so that you feel the new tempo before you play.

Which tempo do you prefer?

Feeling the Rhythm

- Count a pulse of 4/4 and say the words below.
- Say the words while doing the actions.
- "Think" the words while doing the actions.
- Do the actions faster, then slower. How fast or slow can you get and still keep the rhythm?

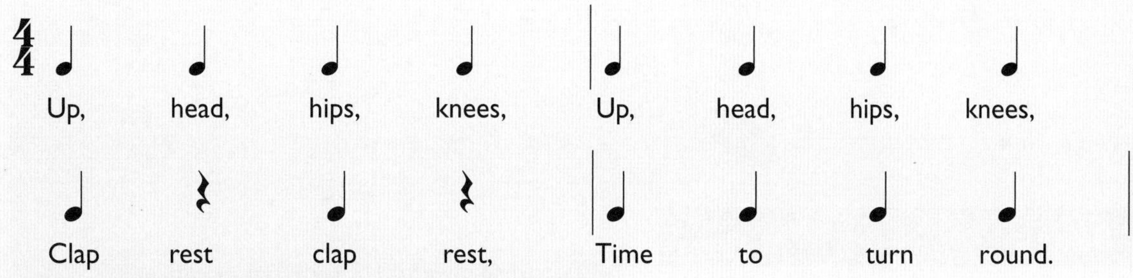

On the word "Up", put your hands in the air.

For the rests, turn your palms upwards.

You could also practise Feeling the Rhythm with track 4 as an accompaniment

Centre Stage

There are two versions of this piece on the CD. What are the differences? Which do you prefer?

Confidently!

Carol Barratt

Playing E

To play **E** extend the slide into second position. To avoid playing **low A**, ensure that your embouchure is firmer and that you provide fast enough air.

This is what **E** looks like written down:

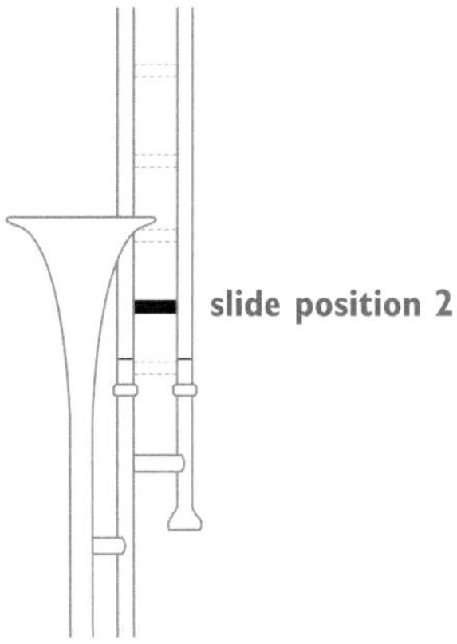

Play or sing **F**, **E♭** and **E** a few times. Which is the highest note and which is the lowest? Can you hear how **E** comes "in between" **F** and **E♭**?

Building Blocks

Using **C**, **D**, **E**, **F** and **G** play these blocks slowly, then a little faster.

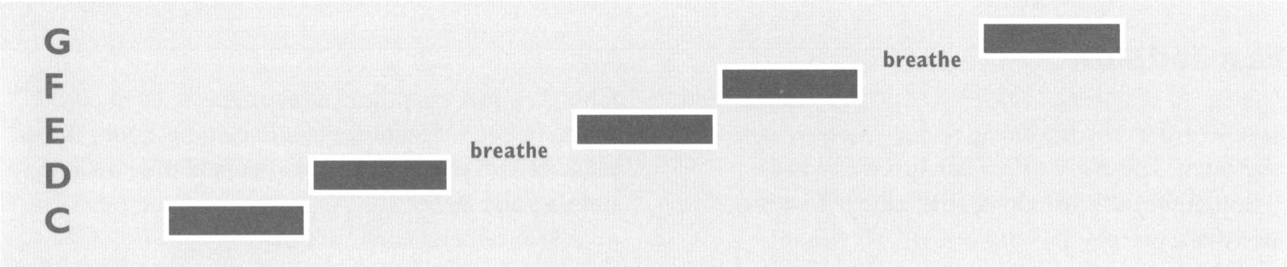

Echo Games

With your teacher, buzz, clap, sing or play these *Echo Games*.

Make up your own Echo Games too.

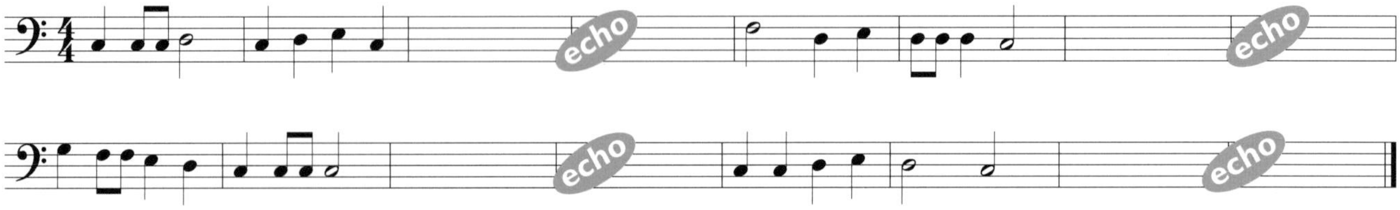

Rags 'n' Bones

Watch out for the natural signs in this piece. Whenever you see **E♮** any following **E♮**s in the same bar without signs are also **E♮**s.

In a piece with a key signature with an E♭, a natural sign in front of the E tells you to play E, not E♭.

With precision

John York

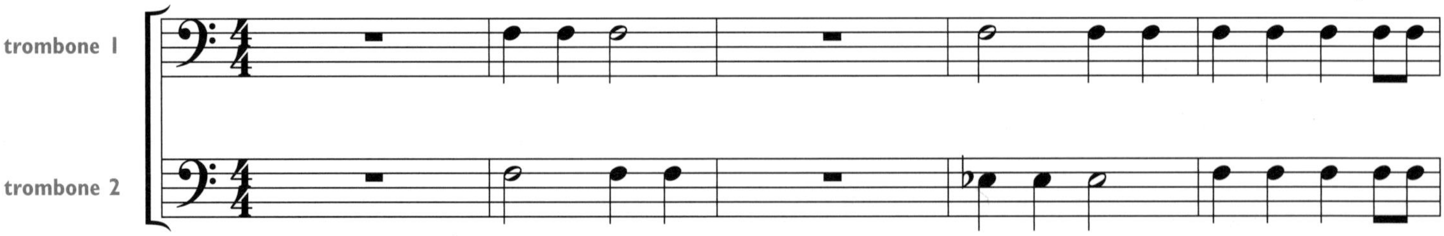

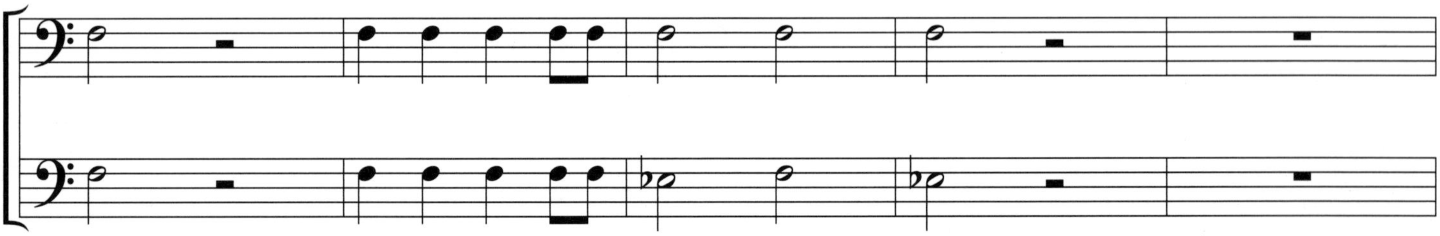

4/4 Rhythm Grid

Look at the rhythms in the grid. You can work across, up or down the grid in any order you like. Using the backing on track 4 as an accompaniment, try the following:

- buzz or clap the rhythms
- sing the rhythms on any note you like
- "think" the rhythms in your head
- play the rhythms using **E**

Can you make up a new tune and learn it from memory?

In and Out

Breathe in		Breathe out				Breathe in		Breathe out			
count		count				count		count			
1	2	1	2	3	4	1	2	1	2	3	4

Spooky Route

Carol Barratt

breathe in quickly and out slowly

51

When the Saints Go Marching in

Can you work out how to play this tune starting on **B♭** not **C**?

Cheerfully traditional

52

Russian Dance

Watch out for the **E♮**s in this piece. Whenever you see an **E♮**, any following **E**s in the same bar without signs are also **E♮**s.

Dmitri Kabalevsky,
arr. Carol Barratt

53

Knights Templar March

Carol Barratt

Make up your own march using **B♭**, **C**, **D** and **E♭** and any rhythms from the grid on the right.

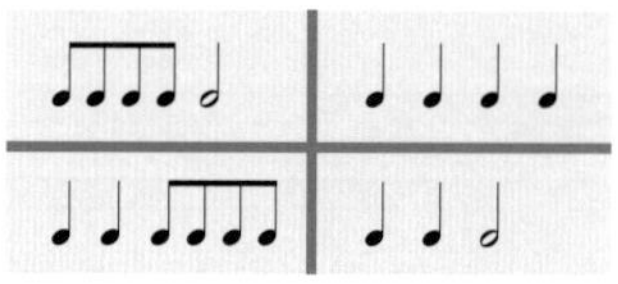

Lip slurs

A slur is when you move between notes smoothly. Passing between two notes which use the same slide position without tonguing the second is a kind of **lip slur**.

Using your mouthpiece only, pass between a higher and lower buzz without tonguing. You could use this exercise as part of your daily warm-up.

Try whistling a low note then a high note. Do you notice what happens to your embouchure?

High Jumps

Play these quite slowly.

- Firstly, tongue both notes of each group.
- Then, tongue the first note of each group only.

When you slur down your lower jaw drops downwards and outwards. This is called a **pivot**.

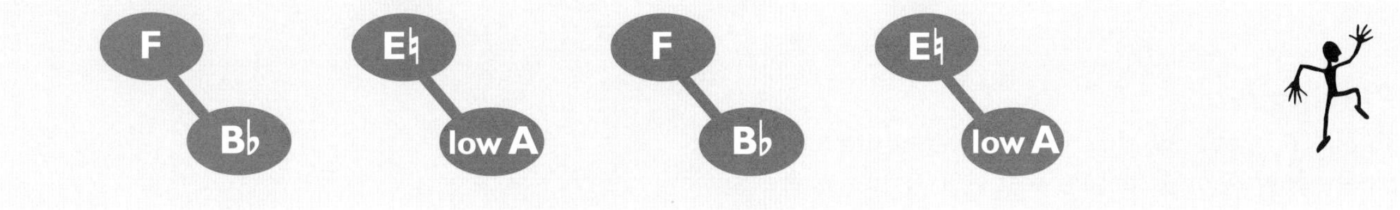

Practise lip slurs between any other notes you know which use the same slide position.

Freewheelin'

Simply

Chris Norton

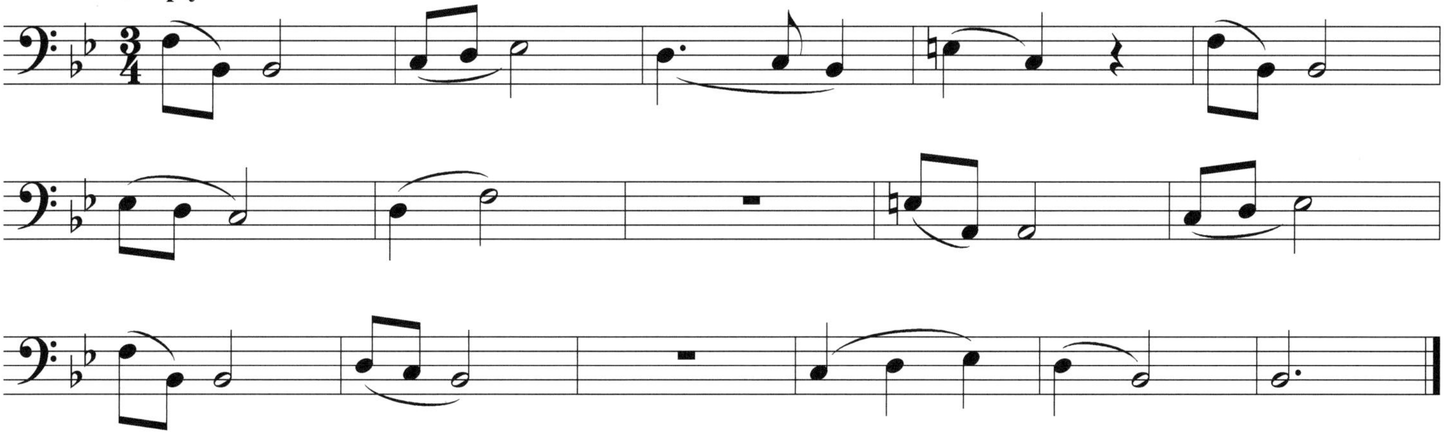

Performance Zone

- Choose some pieces or activities that you could perform for your family or your class. Choose some solos and some pieces to play with others.
- Organise a time and place.
- What will you need? A keyboard, percussion instruments, a CD player, a music stand?
- Can you tell your audience about the pieces you are going to play? You may need to practise this.
- Could someone record the performance?

What went well in your performance? Will you do things differently the next time you perform?

Always use these exercises to warm up before playing any part of Stage 5

Warm-ups

Try the following exercise with and without your mouthpiece only:

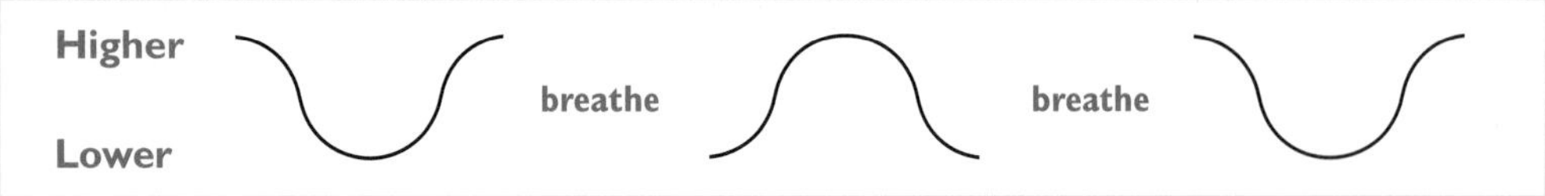

Buzz the following rhythm slowly, then a little faster:

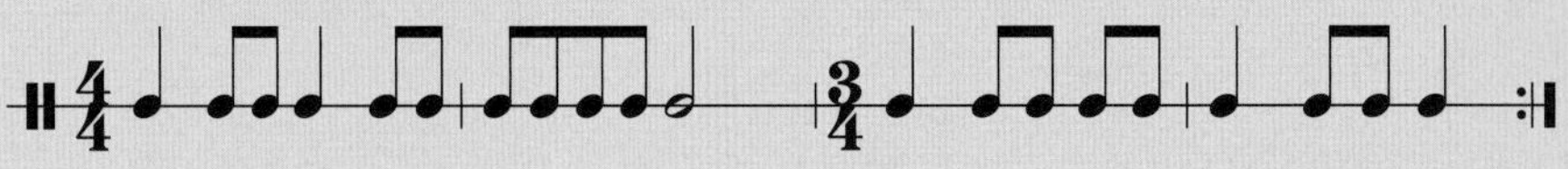

Now play the following *High Jumps*, tonguing the first note of each group. Think of saying 'too' on the first note then 'aah' on the next. Notice how your tongue flattens as your jaw drops downwards.

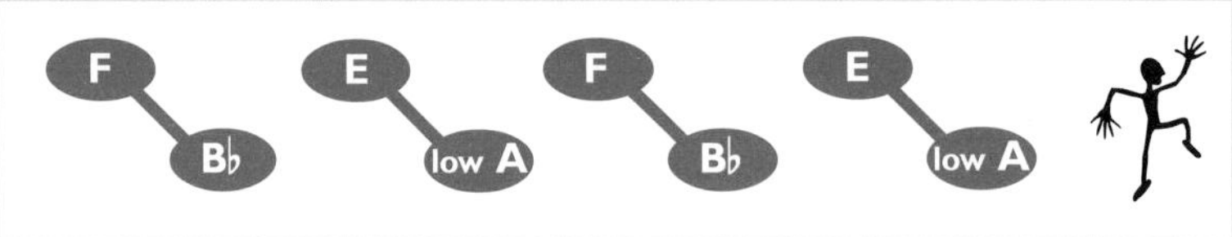

Playing A

To play **A**, move the slide into second position. To avoid playing **low A** or **E**, ensure that your embouchure is firm enough and that the air support is fast enough. This is what **A** looks like written down.

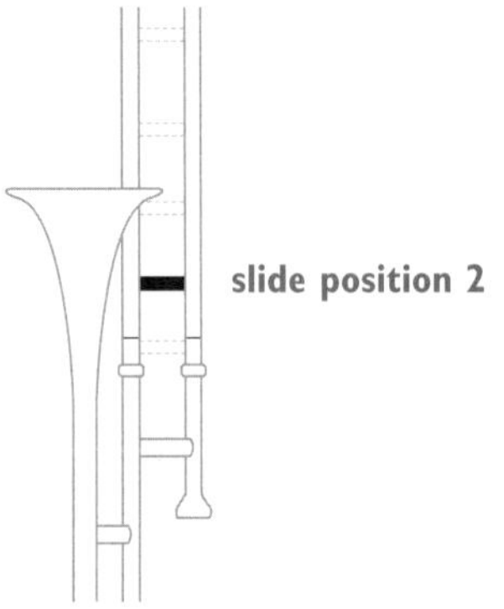

Building Blocks

Using **F**, **G** and **A**, play these blocks slowly, then a little faster.

Try these building blocks with a metronome or with track 4

Make up your own Echo Games too.

Echo Games

With your teacher, buzz the rhythm, clap, sing or play these Echo Games.

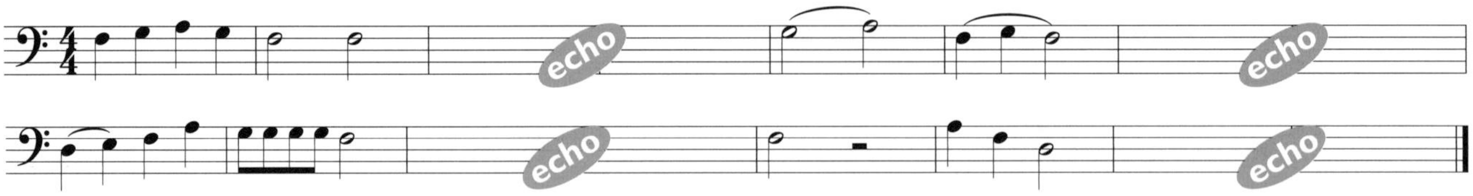

Note Ladders

Choose one rhythm pattern from the grid and use it to play each note in the note ladders. Move up and down the ladders by step.

Clap your rhythm first, then sing the notes of the ladders. Next, "think" notes and the rhythm. Finally, play your ladders.

Then choose another rhythm. Again, clap, sing, think and play the ladders.

Climb up from here...

Little Brown Jug

traditional

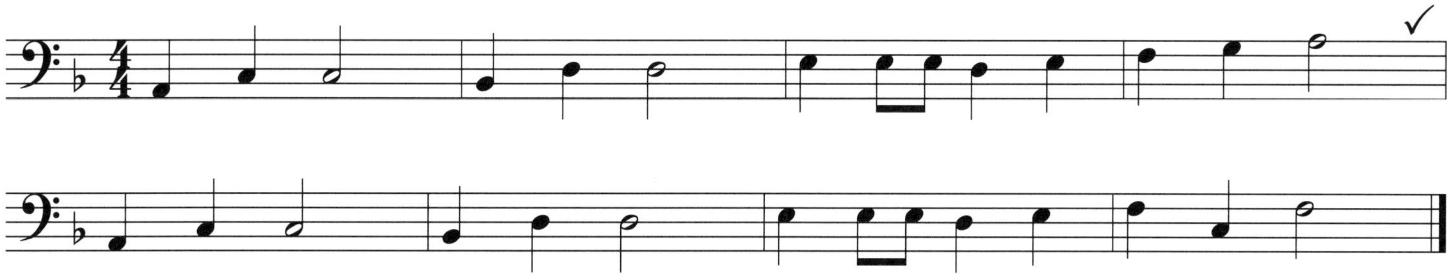

Land of the Silver Birch

Clap, sing, then play. You can play this piece as a round.

A **round** is a piece that can be played by several players, starting at different times. This round is in four parts. The numbers show you when to begin.

traditional Canadian

Feeling the Rhythm

A one-beat note with a dot after it (a dotted crotchet) lasts one and a half beats. Clap or buzz this rhythm, using track 4 of the CD as a pulse.

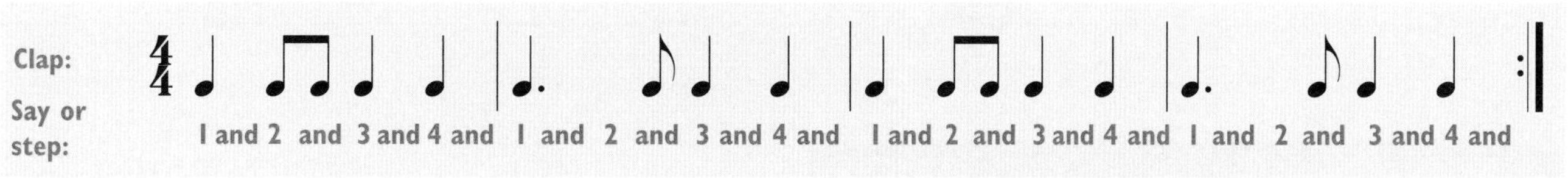

While Shepherds Watched

traditional

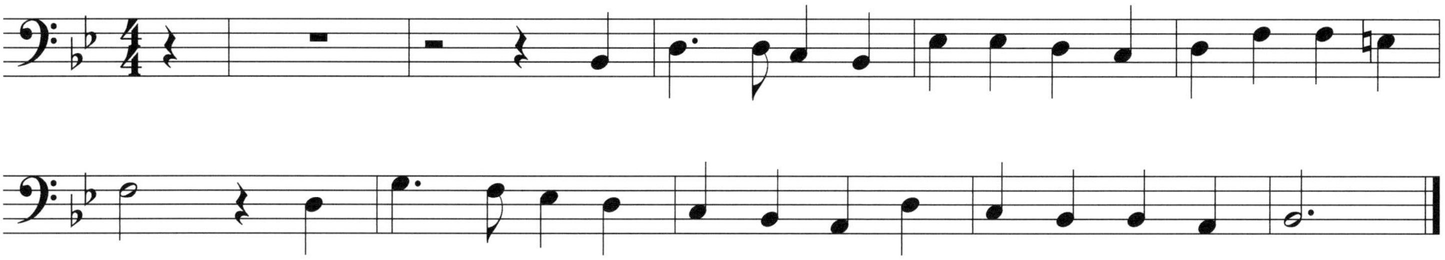

Playing A♭

To play **A♭**, extend the slide into third position. To avoid playing **E♭**, ensure that your embouchure is firm enough and that the air support is fast enough.

This is what **A♭** looks like written down:

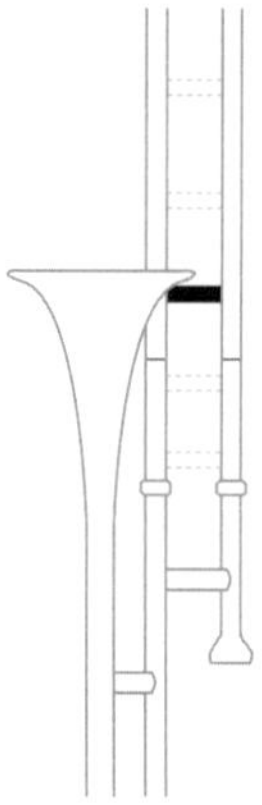

More about flats

Another name for A is A natural.

Play or sing **A**, **G** and **A♭** a few times in any order. Which is the highest note and which is the lowest? Can you hear how **A♭** comes "in between" **A** and **G**?

When a flat sign is in front of A, play A♭.

Building Blocks

Using **F**, **G** and **A♭**, play these blocks slowly, then a little faster.

Echo Games

With your teacher, buzz, clap, sing or play these *Echo Games*.

Make up your own Echo Games too.

Yankee Doodle

58

Remember the key signature in this piece.

traditional American

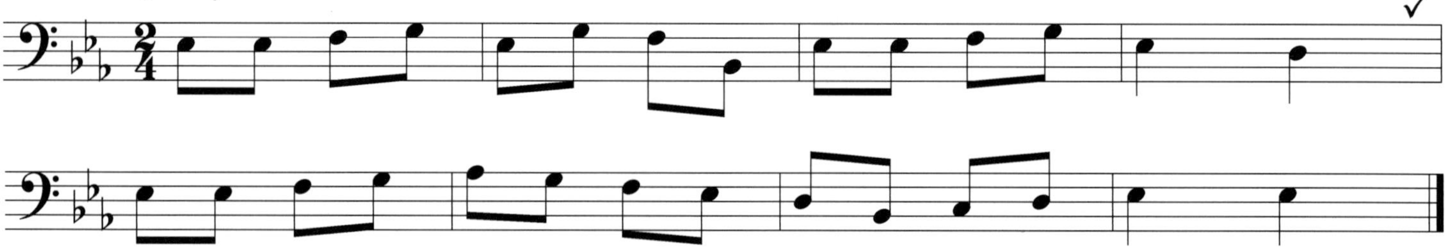

Questions and Answers

- Buzz, clap or play an answer on one note.

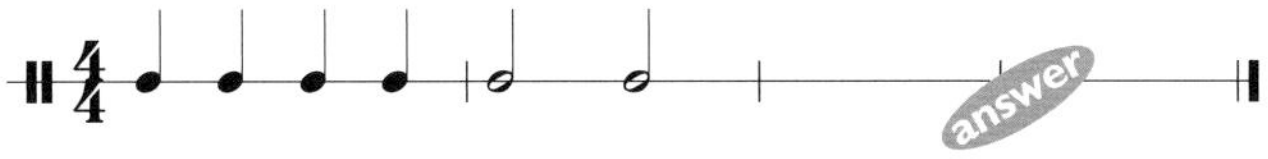

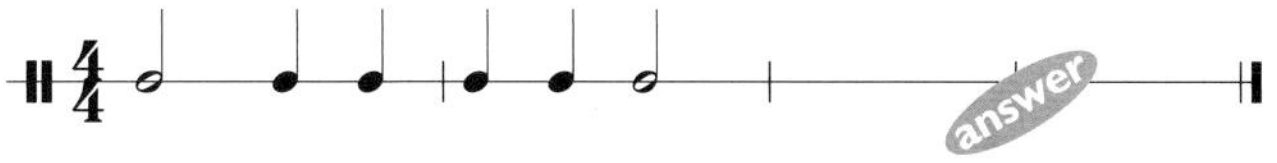

- Play an answer using any notes you know.

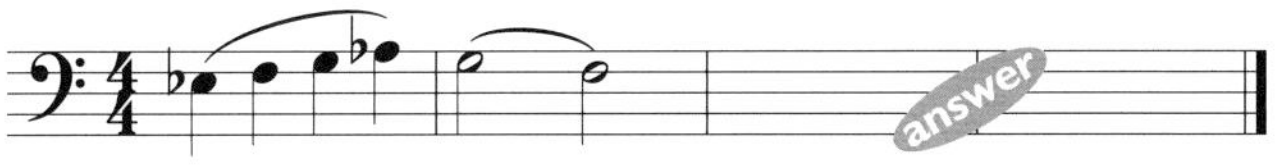

Aura Lee

Learn to play this piece from memory using the practice hints on page 33. Remember the key signature.

Zoom in on the shaded bars.

If you use 6th position to play F, you can practise three different types of slurs in this piece

traditional

Andante

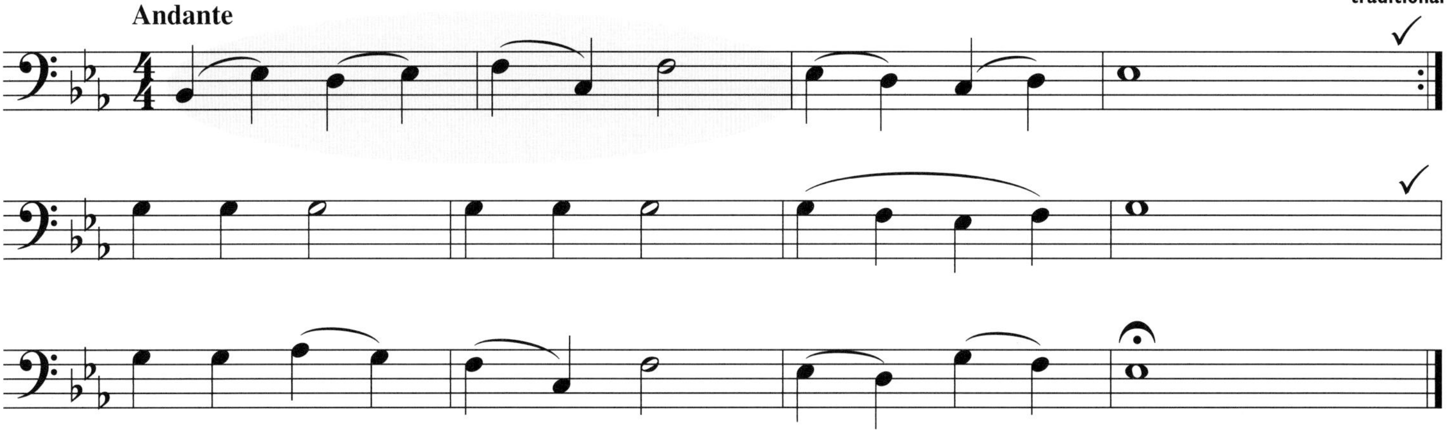

Tall Tale, Big Hat

There are two versions of this piece on the CD. What are the differences? Which do you prefer?

Chris Norton

Urgently

Imaginary Dancer

- Play this piece slowly, keeping to a pulse.
- Then add in the pauses. What length of pause works best for the mood of the piece?
- Then try changes of speed. Decide how much to speed up and how much to slow down.

accel. is short for the Italian word *accelerando*, which means "speed up".

rall. is short for the Italian word *rallentando*, which means "slow down".

Chris Morgan

Play this piece to someone else and see if they feel that your playing helps them to imagine the dancer.

Playing low A♭

Can you play all the notes you know that use slide position 3?

To play **low A♭**, extend the slide to third position. You will also need to relax your embouchure and provide plenty of slow air.

This is what **low A♭** looks like written down:

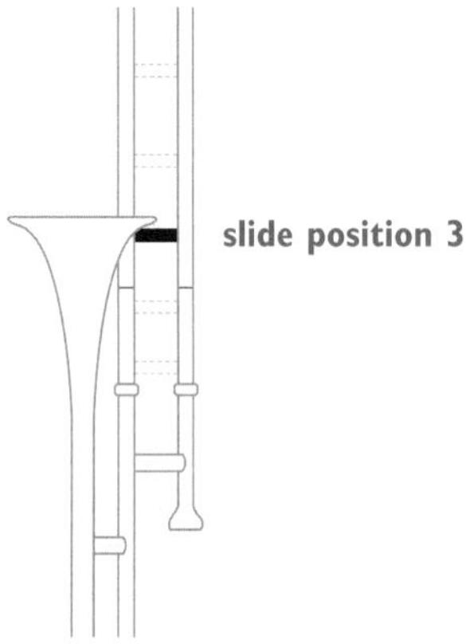

Building Blocks

Using **B♭**, **low A** and **low A♭**, play these blocks slowly, then a little faster.

Echo Games

With your teacher, buzz, clap, sing or play these *Echo Games*.

Make up your own Echo Games too.

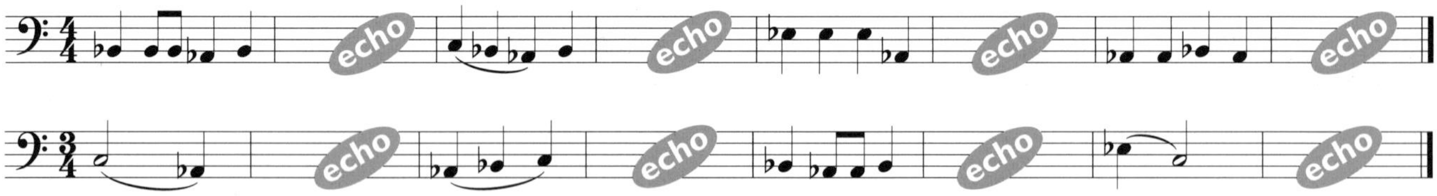

Lopsided

Zoom in on the shaded bar.

Anthony Marks

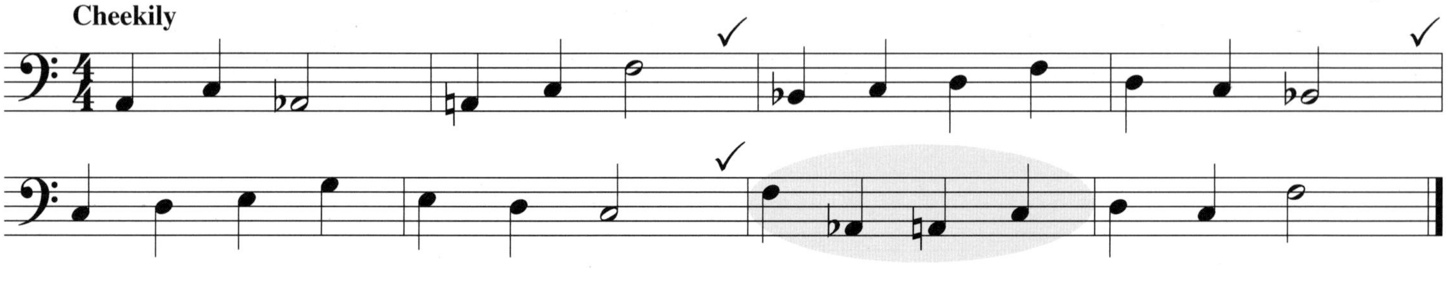

Hopak

Zoom in on the shaded bars. Avoid any tendency to smile, press against the mouthpiece, or strain when playing the slurs.

Carol Barratt

A new time signature

The 5 at the top of this time signature means that there are 5 beats in each bar.

5/4

Feeling the Rhythm

The rhythm below is in 5/4. Clap the first beat of each bar - this will help you feel it as a strong beat. Then add the sounds.

In this rhythm, the words and actions divide each bar into a group of three beats followed by a group of two beats.

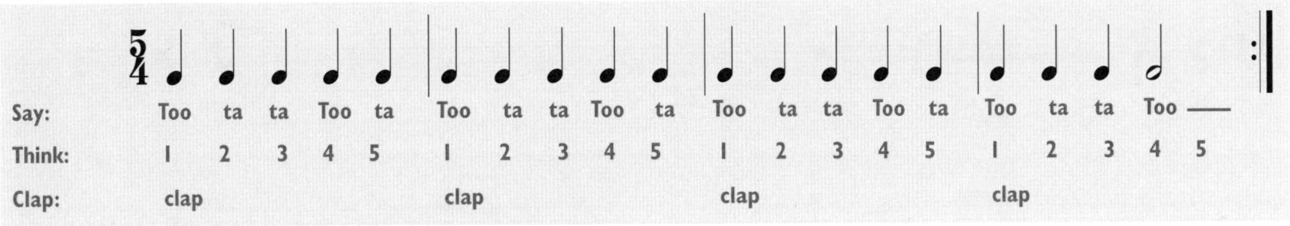

Fanfare Time

Listen to track 64 on the CD and join in after the fanfare.

Play this eight times:

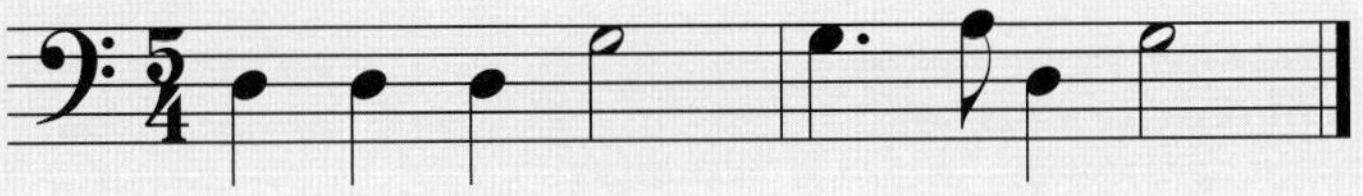

In and Out

Breathe in	Breathe out	Breathe in	Breathe out
count	count	count	count
1 2 3 4 5	1 2 3 4 5	1 2 3 4 5	1 2 3 4 5

65

Upstairs, Downstairs

Play this piece with the slurs, then with each note tongued. Which version do you prefer?

Anthony Marks

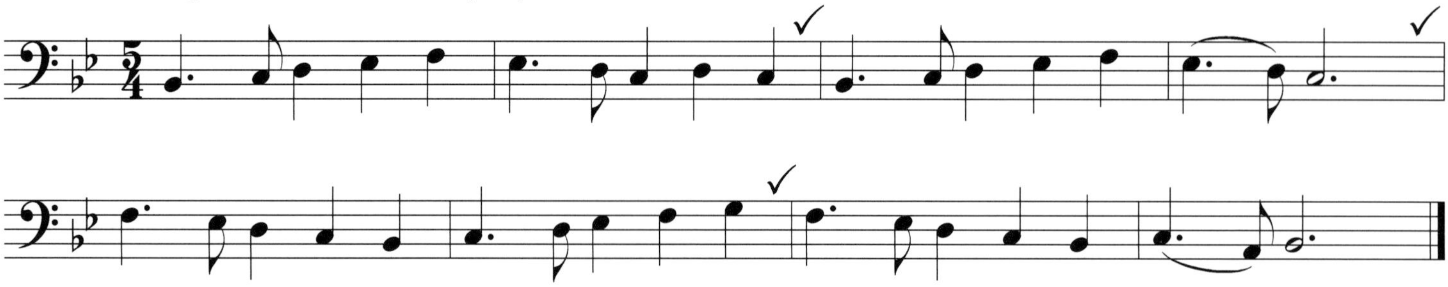

66

Tied up Tight

A curved line joining notes of the same pitch is called a **tie**. Just like a slur, it tells you to join the second note to the first but without soft tonguing it.

Clap, sing, think, then play:

Anthony Marks

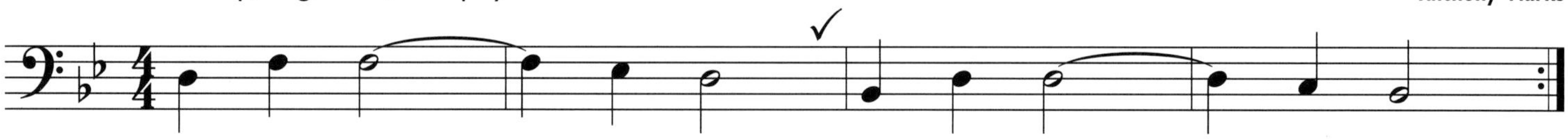

67

Fortune Cookies

Watch out for the tie in the last bar.

Carol Barratt

The Trombone Rap

You can add the following part to your piece. Repeat it as many times as you like. A repeated pattern of notes or rhythms is called an **ostinato**.

You can make *The Trombone Rap* into a longer piece if you add the words on the right. You will need to decide how to say them in rhythm. You could also invent a drum part.

How long will your piece be?

I hear a tune playing, I hear music,
Beats in my feet and the rhythm's begun!
Taking my time to talk in rhyme,
I've got words on the tip of my tongue.

Repeating Patterns

The recording of *The Trombone Rap* on track 68 contains ostinatos (repeating patterns of notes and rhythms). How many can you hear?

1. Invent your own rhythm pattern to go with *The Trombone Rap*. Try lots of different ideas. When you find one you like, write it down.

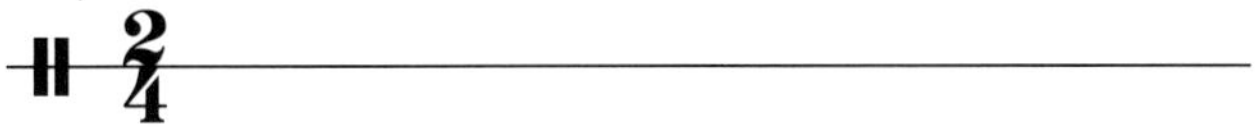

2. Use your pattern as an ostinato.

3. Use your ostinato as an introduction and an ending. When you are happy with your arrangement, make a recording of it.

A new version of a tune is called an arrangement.

Serenade

Zoom in on the shaded bars.

Strong and soft

Most music is loud in some parts and quiet in others. In written music, there are special signs called **dynamics** that tell you how loud or quiet it should be. Play these blocks using **B♭**, then using **F**.

p This sign means "piano", the Italian word for "quietly".

To play quietly, use less air, but make sure the note is supported.

f This sign means "forte", the Italian word for "loudly".

To play loudly, blow *faster*, but make sure the note doesn't "split".

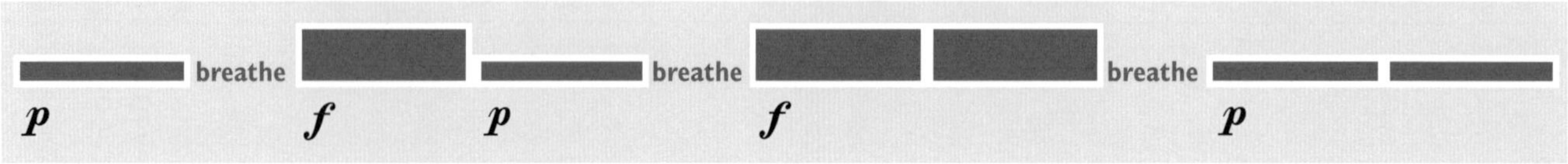

Play some pieces from earlier in the book with a strong sound, then quietly. Which dynamic suits which piece?

Tip-toe

Watch out for the changing time signatures in this piece – count carefully! Zoom in on the shaded bar.

Warm-ups

Always use these exercises to warm up before playing any part of Stage 6

Try the following exercise with and without your mouthpiece only:

On your mouthpiece buzz the following rhythm slowly, then a little faster:

Now play the following *High Jumps* ***p***, tonguing each note. Then play them ***f***, slurring each pair:

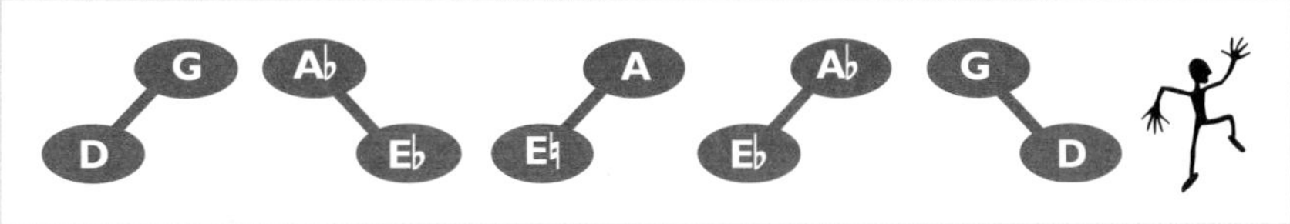

Playing upper B♭

In order to play **upper B♭** and to avoid playing **F** or **lower B♭**, you will need to ensure your embouchure is firm enough and that the air is even faster.

This is what **upper B♭** looks like written down:

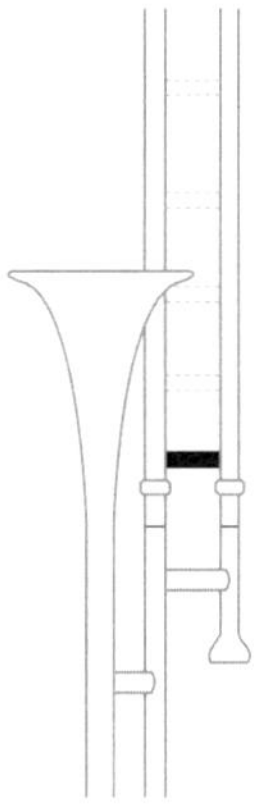

Remember the position of your embouchure and tongue when you whistled a high note (page 37)? This will help.

Building Blocks

Using **B♭**, **F** and **upper B♭**, play these blocks slowly, then a little faster.

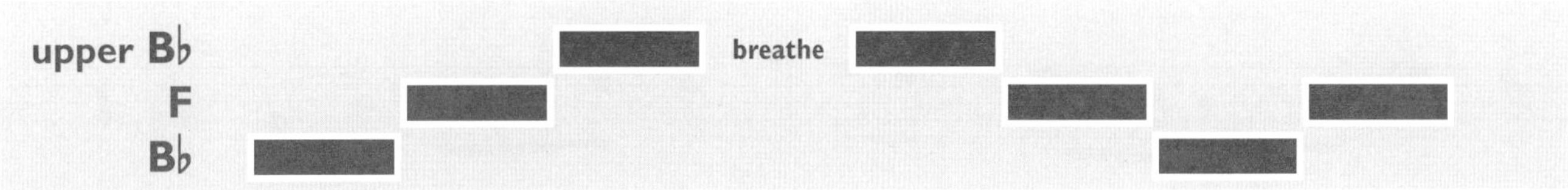

Try these Building Blocks with a metronome or a rhythmic backing track

Now play them using **G**, **A** and **upper B♭**.

High Jumps

Play these quite slowly.

- Tongue each note.
- Slur each group.

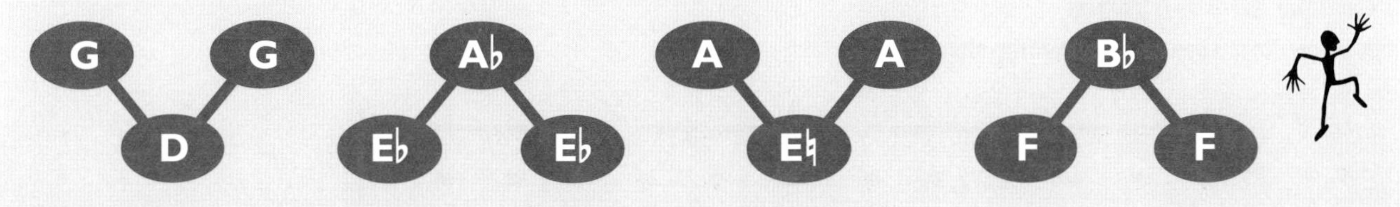

Echo Games

With your teacher, buzz, clap, sing or play these *Echo Games*.

Make up your own Echo Games too.

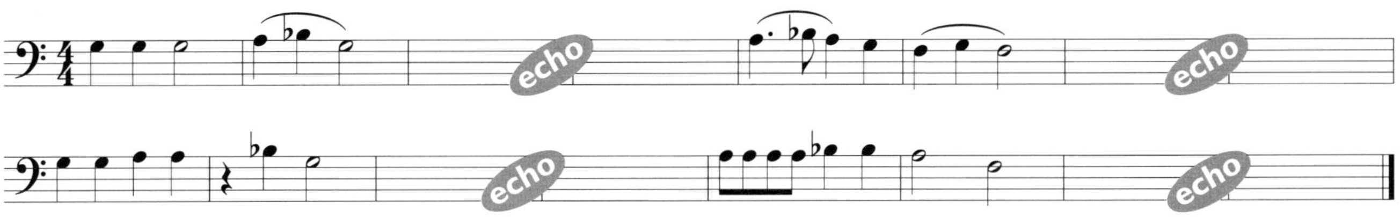

Scales

A group of notes that moves by step is called a **scale**. Scales can start and end on any note.

How many groups of notes that move up by step can you find in *Upstairs, Downstairs* on page 44?

Ski Slopes

- Take the ski-jump up on the left. Create a bumpy take-off by tonguing each note
- Then, imagine that your landing and run down is smooth by slurring the notes on the right.

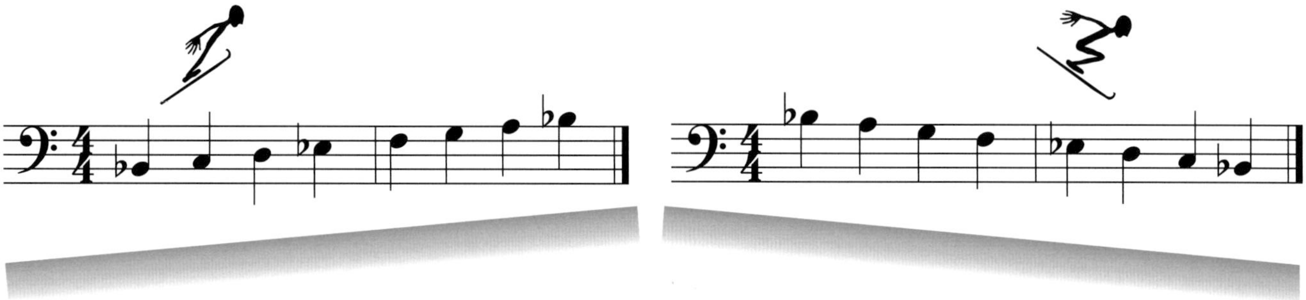

Floral Dance

Play this ***p*** first time through then ***f*** on the repeat. There are two versions of *Floral Dance* on the CD. What are the differences? Which do you prefer?

traditional Cornish

A new time signature

In 6/8, the quavers are in two groups of three, so you count two main beats of dotted crotchets.

6/8 **The 8 at the bottom of this time signature means that the beats are quavers or eighth notes. The 6 tells you that there are 6 of them in each bar.**

Feeling the Rhythm

Clap, say and step the following rhythms:

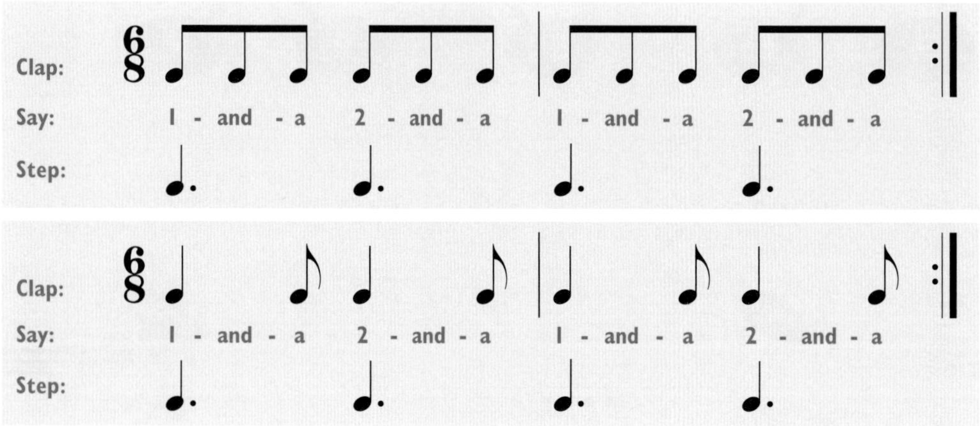

Fanfare Time

Listen to track 72 on the CD and join in after the fanfare.

Play this four times:

In and Out

Breathe in						**Breathe out**					
count						*count*					
1	2	3	4	5	6	1	2	3	4	5	6

Wave Machine

Play this piece using the rhythm on the right too.
mf (*mezzo forte*) tells you to play quite strongly.

etc.

Anthony Marks

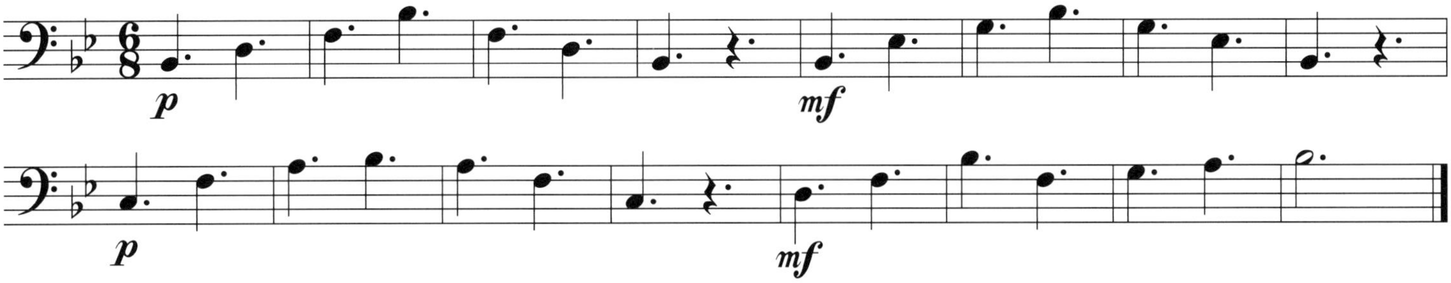

Blaydon Races

traditional English

Questions and Answers

Buzz or clap an answer, or play an answer on one note.

Can you work out how to play a song you have learned at school?

Play an answer using any notes you know.

Level Headed

You can play *Level Headed* as a duet, with the CD or with anyone using a *Boosey Woodwind* or *Boosey Brass* book.

Zoom in on the shaded bars.

This sign is a ***quaver rest*** or ***eighth note rest.*** It lasts for half of one crotchet beat.

Chris Norton

trombone 1

trombone 2

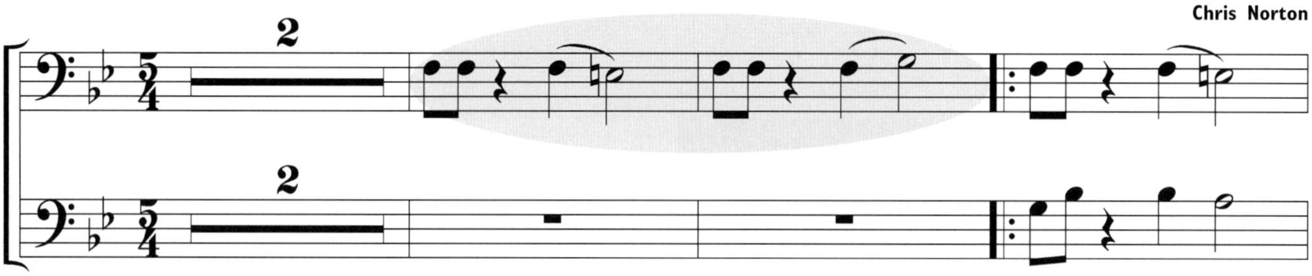

Changing dynamics

Play each *Go-karts* piece as a solo. Then play both together as a duet, starting and finishing each note at the same time.

or *crescendo (cresc.)* means "get louder"

or *diminuendo (dim.)* means "get quieter"

Go-karts, lap one

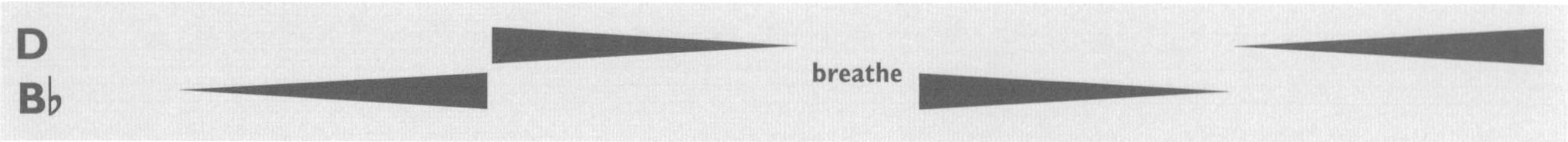

Go-karts, lap two

Shaker Melody

traditional American

Thinking about practising

- Could you play this piece differently – a bit faster or slower, for example? Which speed works best?
- Are you making a clear difference between the loud sections of the piece and the quiet sections?
- Are you making a clear difference between the tongued notes and the slurred notes?
- Record your piece and listen to it. Does it sound as you expected? Will you make any changes next time you play it?

High Jumps

Play these slowly, but breathe where necessary:

- Tongue each note.
- Start at the end and play the notes in reverse order.

Can you get to the end without taking a breath?

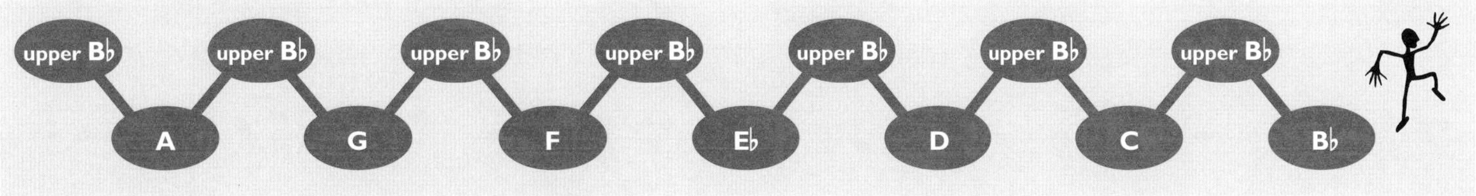

Prelude from Te Deum

Play the dynamics in brackets when you repeat this piece.

Marc-Antoine Charpentier

78

Hine ma tov

Go back to the sign (𝄋) and play until you reach FINE

79

Cool Time

You can arrange *Cool Time* for as many players and singers as you like. All the parts fit together.

Set a pulse with the drum pattern.

Drum pattern

Chris Morgan

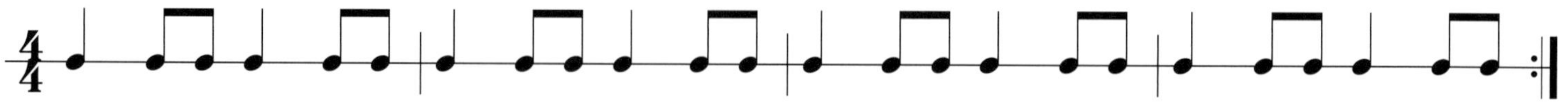

Then add the other parts one by one in any order.

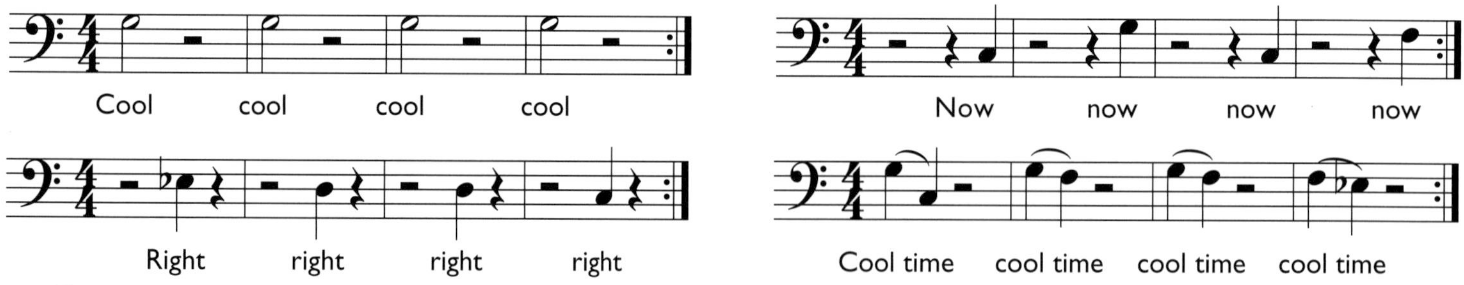

79

Keyboard part

The keyboard part is on track 79 of the CD.

How long will your piece be? Will all the players and singers finish together or in turn?

Write some instructions so that everyone knows when to start and stop. Make a recording too.

Warm-ups

Try this exercise without and with your mouthpiece only:

Buzz the following rhythm slowly, then a little faster:

Now play the following *High Jumps* *p*, tonguing each note. Then play them *f*, slurring each group:

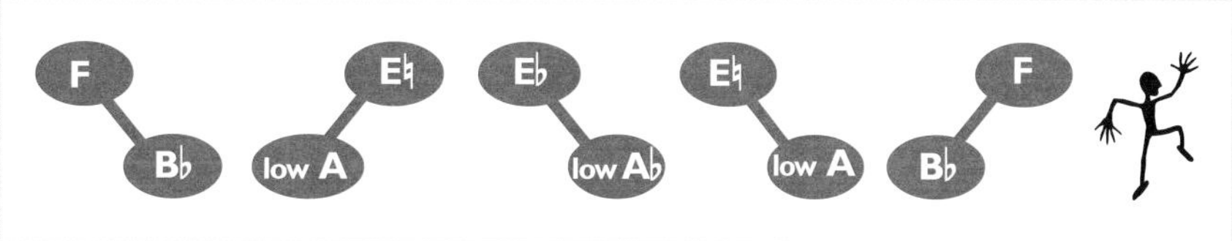

Always use these exercises to warm up before playing any part of Stage 7

Playing low G

To play **low G**, extend the slide into 4th position. To avoid playing **D**, you will also need to relax your embouchure and provide plenty of slow air.

This is what **low G** looks like written down.

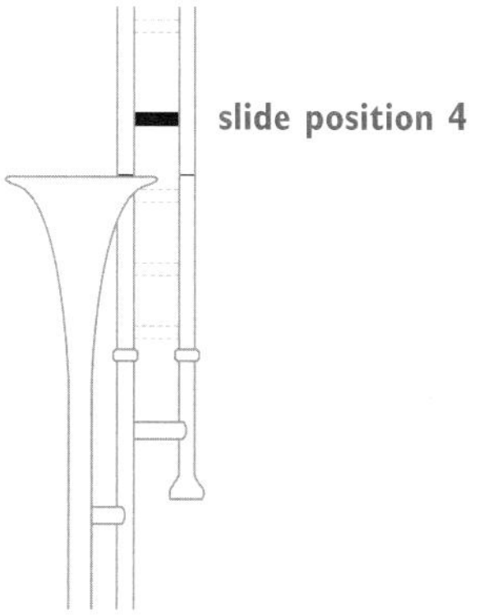

Building Blocks

Play these blocks slowly, then a little faster.

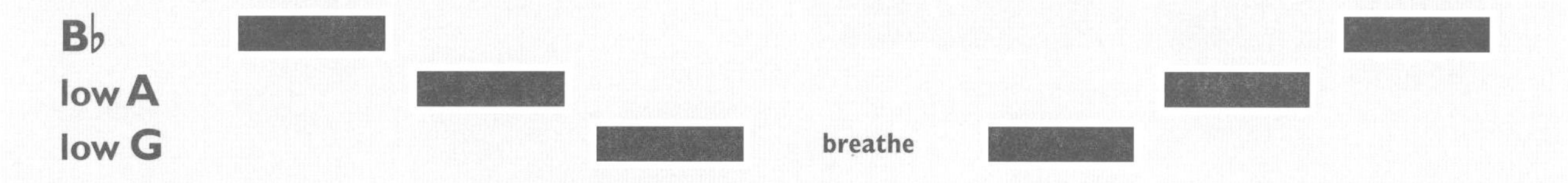

Try these Building Blocks with a metronome or a rhythmic backing track

Echo Games

With your teacher, buzz, clap, sing or play these *Echo Games*.

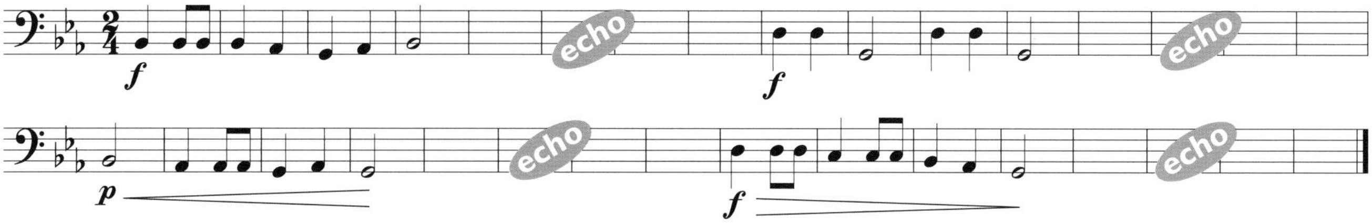

Make up your own Echo Games too.

Blue 4 U

80
81

There are two versions of *Blue 4 U* on the CD. What are the differences? Which do you prefer?

You could also play this with a drum pattern on an electronic keyboard. Which style setting works best?

Anthony Marks

L'homme armé

A round is explained on *page 39*

This is an old French tune. The title means "The armed man". It can be played as a round. Try it in two parts, with the second person joining in after two bars, then after four bars, and so on. Try it with three parts, or four. Which version works best?

traditional

In and Out

Breathe in				Breathe out							
count				count							
1	2	3	4	1	2	3	4	5	6	7	8

Mayim! Mayim!

Zoom in on the shaded bars.

traditional Jewish

Questions and Answers

Can you work out how to play a theme from a soap opera?

Buzz or clap an answer or play an answer on one note.

Play an answer using any notes.

Kalinka

This is a Russian folk song. When you know this piece, play it without the CD a bit faster. How fast can you play and still keep the rhythm steady?

Experiment with pauses of different lengths. Which length works best?

84

traditional Russian

A Groovy Kind of Love

Zoom in on the shaded bars.

85

Toni Wine & Carole Bayer Sager

Penguins on Toast

A dot above or below a note tells you to cut it short, leaving a tiny gap before the next note. This is called **staccato**.

Charming

You can play this piece as a duet, with the CD, or with anyone using a *Boosey Woodwind* or *Boosey Brass* book.

Chris Norton

Warm-ups

Try this exercise without and with your mouthpiece only. Tongue each block separately, then slur them.

On your mouthpiece, buzz the following rhythm slowly, then a little faster.

Always use these exercises to warm up before playing any part of Stage 8

Now play the following *High Jumps* ***p***, tonguing each note. Then play them ***f***, slurring each group.

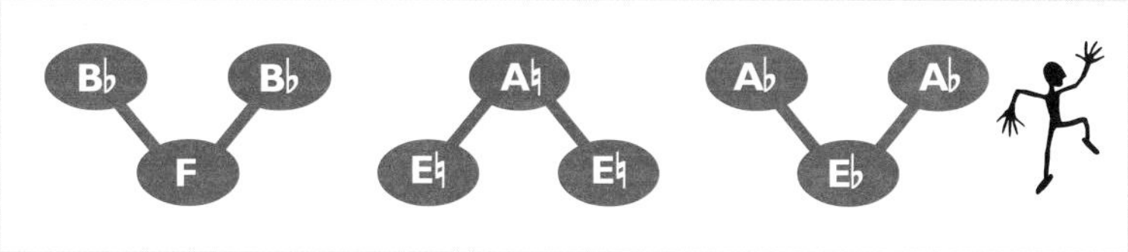

Playing upper B and upper C

To play **upper B** extend the slide into fourth position. **Upper C** is in third position. To play both notes you will need to ensure your embouchure is firm enough and that the air support is even faster.

This is what **upper B** and **upper C** look like written down:

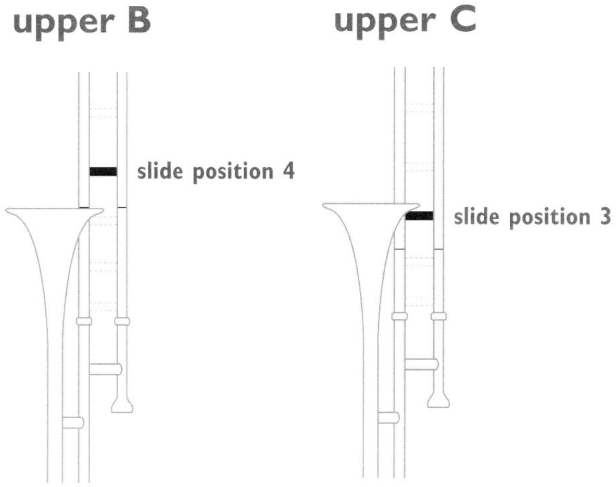

Can you think of any other notes which use the same slide positions and also move by semitone?

Building Blocks

Play these blocks slowly, then a little faster.

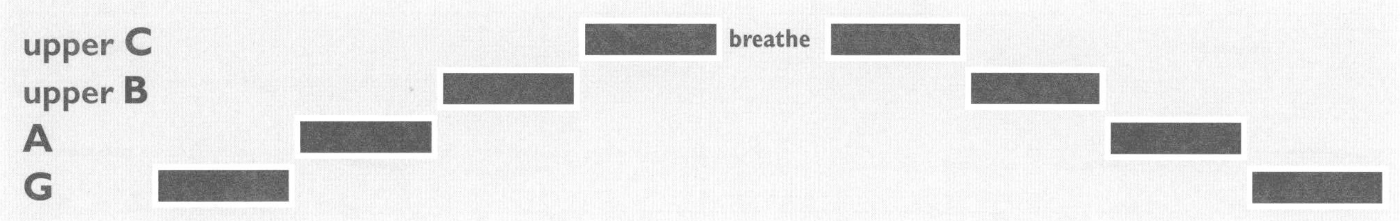

Try these Building Blocks with a metronome or a rhythmic backing track

Echo Games

With your teacher, buzz the rhythm, clap, sing or play these Echo Games.

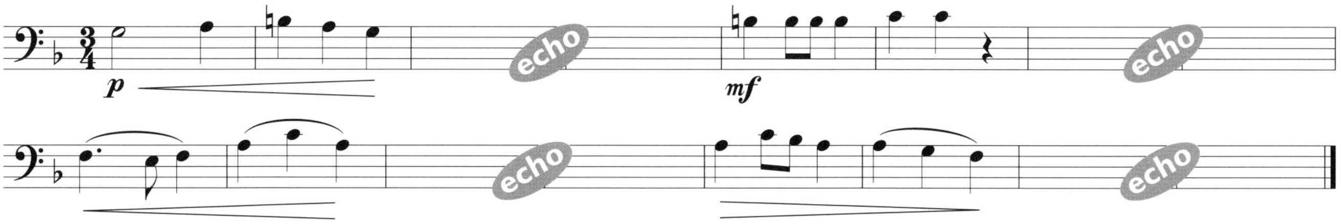

Make up your own Echo Games too.

In and Out

Take a deep breath in, then breathe out slowly.

Breathe in	Breathe out	Breathe in	Breathe out
count	*count*	*count*	*count*
1 2	1 2 3 4 5 6 7 8	1 2	1 2 3 4 5 6 7 8

87

Swing Low, Sweet Chariot

This tune is a spiritual. Spirituals are Christian songs which were originally sung by slaves.

traditional

88
89

Hélas madame

There are two versions of *Hélas madame* on the CD. What are the differences? Which do you prefer?

This piece is a duet. If you are playing on your own, play the top part.

Optional drum pattern:

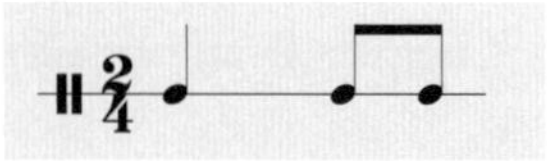

attrib. Henry VIII,
arr. Carol Barratt

Bouncy

Cantilena

This tune is taken from *Adiemus* by Karl Jenkins.
Cantilena means "a little song".

Karl Jenkins

Feeling the Rhythm

Some notes begin and end "in between" the beats. Rhythms containing notes like this are called **syncopations**. Clap the rhythms below.

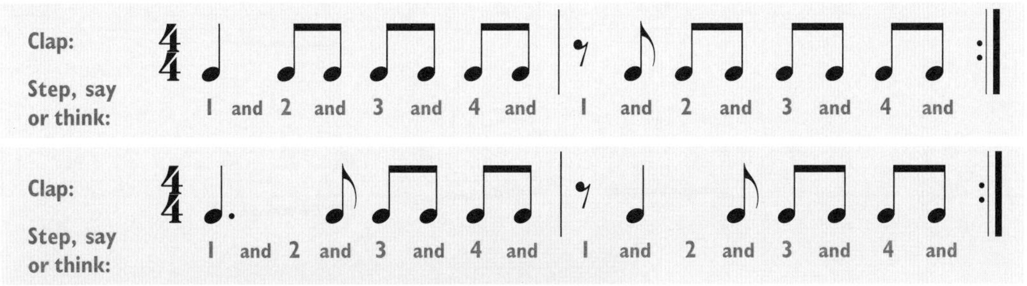

Dodi li

Dodi li is a love song from the Old Testament. *D.S. al Coda* tells you to go back to the sign (𝄋) then when you reach the coda sign (⊕), go straight to the coda.

Nira Chen

Using your mouthpiece only, see if you can make a sound like a siren. How high and low can you go?

High Jumps

Try these High Jumps:

- ***f*** tongued
- ***p*** slurred

Athol Highlander's Jig

Zoom in on the shaded bars.

traditional Scottish

Prince of Denmark's March

Jeremiah Clarke

With spirit

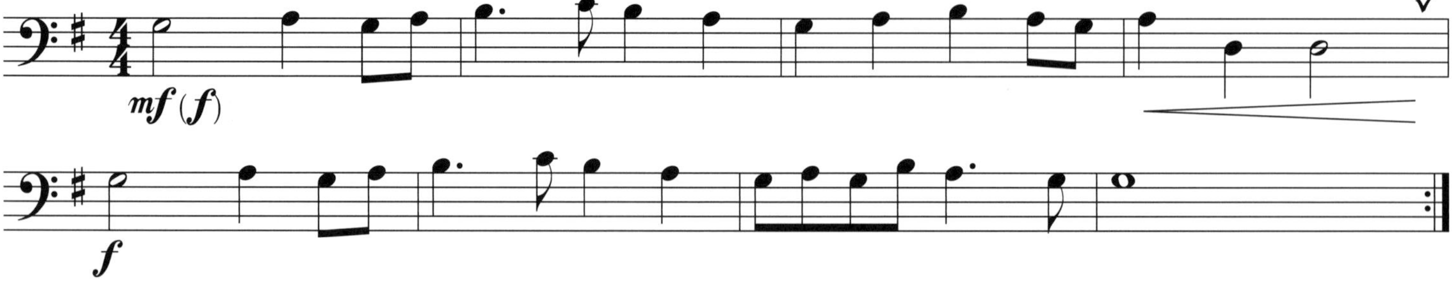

Playing, Practising, Performing

Play *Prince of Denmark's March* in different ways:

- Play it slower, then faster.
- Play with different dynamics.
- Add slurs of different lengths.

Choose pieces from earlier in the book and try them in different ways. When you make new versions of pieces, which do you prefer?

Image

John York & Anthony Marks

Do it Yourself!

Image was written to sound like a television theme tune. What sort of programme could it introduce? What would it work best for, and why? If you made it faster or slower, or louder or quieter, would it still work as well?

Invent your own short jingle or theme for a TV or radio show.

- What kind of programme it is for? Is it serious? Funny? Dramatic? Frightening?
- How will you capture its mood?
- Is it for trombone solo or for more than one instrument?

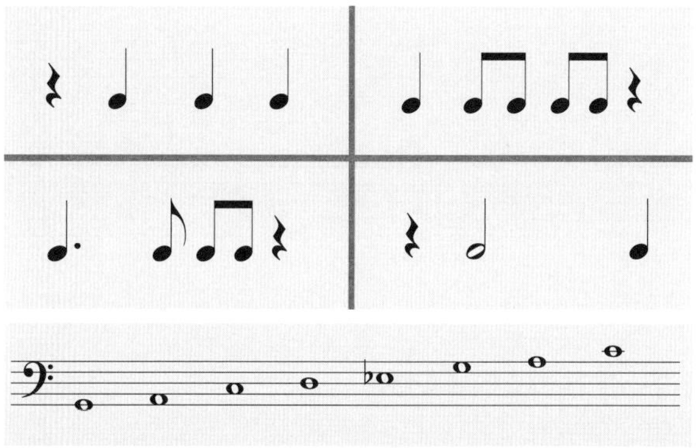

You could use the notes and rhythms in the grid above, or any others that you know.

Can you work out how to play your favourite TV theme tune?

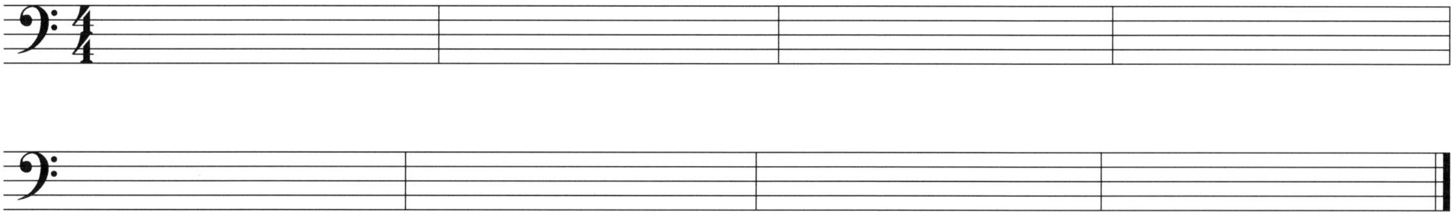

A Life on the Ocean Wave

Henry Russell

Pastime with Good Company

Henry VIII

Performance Zone

Put on a show! Here are some tips:

- Decide where you would like to perform and contact the person in charge. Arrange a time for the performance.
- Design some posters to advertise your concert. Where will you put them? Will you need to make some tickets? Arrange for someone to record the performance too.
- Choose what to play. Use anything from this book, or any other pieces you know. Include your own arrangements or compositions, too. If you want to perform duets and trios, have you got enough musicians for the concert?
- Decide what you are going tell the audience about the music. And practise taking a bow!

Tragic Consequences

You can play this piece as a duet, with the CD, or with anyone using a *Boosey Woodwind* or *Boosey Brass* book.

Chris Norton

Fanfare Time

Finally, here is the tune from the first piece in this book.

Chris Norton

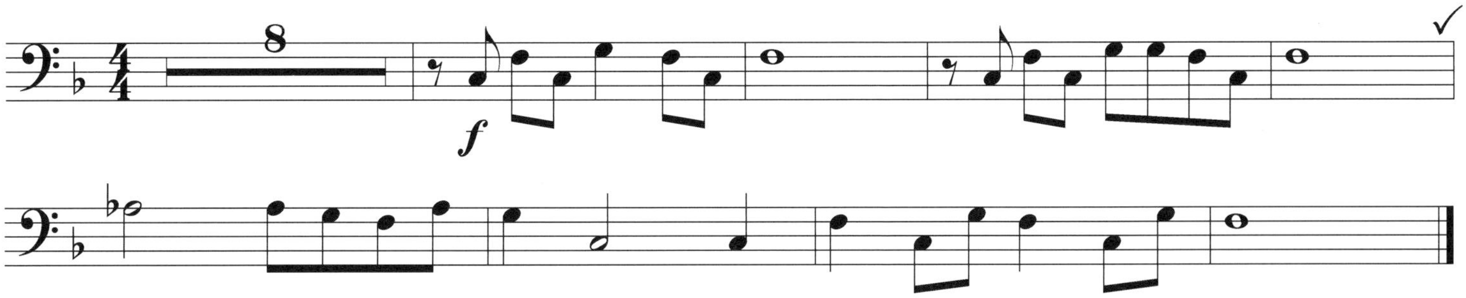

CHECKLISTS

Below are checklists for each stage of this book. As you work through each stage, it may help you to put a tick by each activity as you do it. Make sure you have completed most of the activities in one stage before you move onto the next. When you have completed all the stages, you are ready for Book 2!

Stage 1 - ✔ when you have:

❍ practised *Warm-ups*

❍ played *Starting Blocks* using F

❍ practised *Feeling the Rhythm* with the actions

❍ listened to some music and counted groups of beats

❍ practised *In and Out*

❍ played some *Echo Games*

❍ used the practice hints (clap, sing, think, play) to play *Summer Song*

❍ practised the shaded bar in *Shore to Sea*

❍ played a duet

❍ made some *Questions and Answers*

❍ learned at least six pieces

Stage 2 - ✔ when you have:

❍ practised *Warm-ups*

❍ played some *Echo Games*

❍ made some *Questions and Answers*

❍ practised the shaded bar in *Awesome*

❍ invented your own piece using D, E♭, F and G

❍ practised *Feeling the Rhythm*

❍ practised In and Out

❍ made up your own *Note Grid*

❍ played *Note Ladders* using different rhythms

❍ learned at least six pieces

Stage 3 - ✔ when you have:

❍ practised *Warm-ups*

❍ played some *Echo Games*

❍ practised the shaded bar in *Lazy Days*

❍ made up your own *Note Grid*

❍ practised *In and Out*

❍ compared two versions of *Calm Sea*

❍ made some *Questions and Answers*

❍ learned at least six pieces

Stage 4 - ✔ when you have:

❍ practised *Warm-ups*

❍ played some *Echo Games*

❍ made some *Questions and Answers*

❍ compared two versions of *Mattachins*

❍ played *Lightly Row* from memory

❍ played a piece at two different speeds

❍ practised *In and Out*

❍ made up a march

❍ completed *Performance Zone*

❍ learned at least six pieces

Stage 5 - ✔ when you have:

❍ practised *Warm-ups*

❍ played some *Echo Games*

❍ played *Land of the Silver Birch* as a round

❍ practised *Feeling the Rhythm*

❍ made some *Quesions and Answers*

❍ compared two versions of *Tall Tale, Big Hat*

❍ played *Fanfare Time*

❍ made your own version of *The Trombone Rap*

❍ played pieces from earlier stages using different dynamics

❍ learned at least six pieces

Stage 6 - ✔ when you have:

❍ practised *Warm-ups*

❍ played *High Jumps*

❍ practised *Feeling the Rhythm*

❍ played *Fanfare Time*

❍ played *Wave Machine* with different rhythms

❍ played made some *Questions and Answers*

❍ played *Go-karts* as a duet

❍ tried different ways of practising *Shaker Melody*

❍ made an arrangement of *Cool Time*

❍ learned at least six pieces

Stage 7 - ✔ when you have:

❍ practised *Warm-ups*

❍ played some *Echo Games*

❍ compared the two versions of *Blue 4 U*

❍ played *L'homme Armé* as a round

❍ made some *Questions and Answers*

❍ experimented with pauses in *Kalinka*

❍ practised *In and Out*

❍ learned at least six pieces

Stage 8 - ✔ when you have:

❍ practised *Warm-ups*

❍ played some *Echo Games*

❍ practised *In and Out*

❍ played both parts of *Hélas Madame*

❍ practised syncopation in *Feeling the Rhythm*

❍ played *High Jumps*

❍ played *Prince of Denmark's March* in different ways

❍ invented a theme or jingle for a TV or radio show

❍ completed *Performance Zone*

❍ played *Fanfare Time*

❍ learned at least six pieces